C000200701

MEANS OF ESCAPE

by the same author

non-fiction
INISHKILLANE:
Change and Decline in the West of Ireland

MAPS AND DREAMS

LIVING ARCTIC

NINETEEN NINETEEN
(with Michael Ignatieff)

Hugh Brody
MEANS
OF ESCAPE

faber and faber

LONDON · BOSTON

For Marijia Faust

First published in Canada in 1991 by Douglas & McIntyre
First published in Great Britain in 1991
by Faber and Faber Limited
3 Queen Square London WC1N 3AU

Printed in England by Clays Ltd, St Ives plc

All rights reserved

© Hugh Brody, 1991

Hugh Brody is hereby identified as author of this work
in accordance with Section 77 of the Copyright,
Designs and Patents Act 1988.

A CIP record for this book
is available from the British Library

ISBN 0–571–16488–9

2 4 6 8 10 9 7 5 3 1

CONTENTS

Acknowledgements   6

Family Trees   7

Eva   29

Island   81

The Lake   141

Wolf   173

Acknowledgements

We tell stories to make sense of our lives, in order to visit inner chambers. But the inner chambers look out onto vistas of the real world.

When I sent the stories in this book to friends and publishers for comments, when I broke the solitude, I heard voices — more implicit than explicit — which said to me, somewhat accusingly: this is not fiction, I know where this comes from. The voices — more explicit than implicit — also said: these stories are about the author, so you must declare yourself.

Since every writer hopes that the solitude from which the work emerges illuminates, let me make myself as plain as possible.

Many, many thousands — perhaps millions — live now with the eruptive pain of our parents' and grandparents' dispossession. Holocausts, like nuclear fallout, poison the coming generations. And many, many thousands search for a peace that they imagine will come from a sense of place. Then we discover that peace and place have themselves fallen victim, have been irradiated. But the search, even for absences, does not then cease.

The stories in this book (and my hope is that they will be read in their sequence here) represent the findings of a one-person search party. Those who have made similar journeys — to the far north, to the unconscious, to adulthood, to Scotland, to the cold wars of global and personal politics, to central Europe, to fear — will no doubt be able to say, at times: this is not fiction. Some may recognize a scene from near the end of "Eva." Others may have visited the places I go in "The Lake." And they, too, may say: this is not fiction.

But it is. There is no such person as Aunt Sonia. My solitudes might be in this book. My story is not.

Fiction is not, of course, an escape.

Many friends have supported this work. In particular I want to thank Yvonne Barlow, Anthony Barnett, John Berger, Lorraine Brooke, Patrick Costelo, Arnold Cragg, Anne Cubitt, Caroline Goldie, Hannele Halm, Marcie Jackman, Heather Jarman, Bill Kemp, Margaret Myers, Leslie Pinder and Miranda Tufnell.

FAMILY
TREES

She arrived with a great clamour of hugs and shouts that was followed by a peculiar quiet. She settled herself into the spare room — hardly more than a narrow bed and a dressing table with a jar of flowers. Aunt Sonia had come for her summer visit.

Each year she said to me: "You are my favourite relative."

So I sat for some part of every day of every August, on a Persian rug that served as a bedspread, in her tight little room with a view over an English suburb.

What did Aunt Sonia look like to us children? She seemed so large, so grand, so loud, so important. Her bedspread was so dense with intricate perfection. Her clothesbrush, set out beside a cigarette case on the dressing table, was silver backed. I had a sense of immaculacy and riches. A wonderful superiority.

She gave informal lessons in who we all were. "I'm going to tell you about cousin Olga. An artist. The voice of an angel. She was the best — of Vienna, Berlin, Warsaw." Her authority was unquestionable.

Her voice had a complete intensity: the sounds concentrated and unfamiliar, the emphases extreme and unexpected. Fifteen years later I realized that she had a heavy central European accent.

She said: "You must represent me, you understand? You must be my representative in this English-speaking world."

She urged me, without ever saying the words, never to forget that *real* civilization came from a world which had been effaced.

She said: "You must learn to see the invisible. You must search always for those who have been disappeared."

She insisted that English was not quite a language of real culture. "Certainly not since Shakespeare!" And I sometimes got the impression from her that Shakespeare read better in German translation. "But now," she said, "after all that has been said in German, with the war, we can no longer regard German as a decent language." Still, she told me there were words in German that could not be found elsewhere. These, she said, we must understand. So particular words — Schadenfreude, Weltanschauung, Gemütlichkeit — broke into her English like exotic birds. Magnificent, somehow ominous for their perfection, and — to me — incomprehensible.

She said: "You must speak to me in French. To overcome the disability of Englishness." I agreed: since she did the talking, I was not much tested. My French lessons began with little commands. "Ouvre la fenêtre." "Une cigarette, s'il te plaît." These sounds seemed to be full of beauty and truth (I knew what they meant!), and added to my childish belief that one's own language, the original language, holds very little of that which *must* be understood.

The historical silences of our home were broken each summer by little more than the use of a rather fractious German. I remember that everyone cursed the cat with the particularly inappropriate "Jesus-Maria!" Adults spoke German when they thought it best the children not understand. They may have exchanged in this secret code a multitude of thoughts and anecdotes about that other, ornate home deep behind their eyes. But I doubt it. I suspect that they used German to mention chocolates that were rationed or things that propriety, not suffering, deemed better concealed.

These summers of childhood faded behind webs of growing up, and with the inevitable moves out of small rooms and away from strange, warm sounds or the cursing of the cat. In a way, in the way that is the nature of growing older, I forgot who Aunt Sonia was.

Then, many years later, after decades of forgetful travel, I returned to London. Now, with children of my own, I wondered what had become of Aunt Sonia. Suddenly I wanted to reach across all the times and distances between me and my antecedents. As if, in knowing more of the origins, the present would make better sense. As if, by visiting her again, in whatever room, I could set my own children — or the child in myself — on firm ground.

I wrote her a note, and suggested we meet. She replied with an invitation to tea. She gave me directions: turn left outside the underground station at a northwest corner of the District Line, left again, and look for the house with five rose bushes and an iron gate.

As a child I had imagined her home in London to be as splendid, as ornate and unquestionable, as she herself. But behind the gate and the rose bushes was a drab, suburban maisonette.

She welcomed me at the door and led me to a tiny kitchen where she pressed me to eat central European delicacies. She talked about plays she had seen on television and articles in newspapers. She spoke with all the passion, with all the accents, of the European émigré. And I listened for echoes.

How natural it seemed to sit there. The comfort of family ties without their customary reproaches. I visited often.

I discovered that she was very small, very compact. Her clothes were always neat, enclosing her firmly. Her hair was grey and set in a wave. She wore a patch of powdery pink on each cheek, and thin lines of lipstick. I realized that she was an energetic, impatient woman. And bossy, too. Not someone for whom a mellow nostalgia or pained dredging through the past was anything like a habit. Far from it: she buried events under the energies of today. I asked her questions about her life, but she refused to return to the Europe of her childhood. She said: "I was twenty-five when I left Vienna, a few weeks after the German Anschluss." And she told me: "I would never again set foot in those parts of the world!"

She talked about characters in her life, but apart from their history. She avoided any real journey into prewar days. Nonetheless, I began to feel I could look through her eyes at footprints leading to and from the history that, in some measure, was also my own. And one day I asked her if she kept any old pictures of herself when young, the house they had lived in, Vienna before the war. She pulled a box from the back of a cupboard: a collection of photographs — a tattered archaeology of her life and culture.

All of the pictures in the collection predated the war, and none of their subjects had ever cared to visit England. They included oval portraits and groups by the sea. Self-conscious but often full of laughter: bright and various forms of another era's here and now.

Among the photographs I found in Aunt Sonia's archaeological box was a tiny portrait of my great-grandmother. I asked if I could keep it. "Of course," said Aunt Sonia. "Take any of them." But I took just the one, and put it in my wallet. I never knew my great-grandmother. My desire to have her photograph may have come from a need to carry the image that reached furthest back in family time.

The picture's quality is surprisingly good: a large, pale woman squints out of a backdrop of studio clouds. At first glance her expression appears severe; a closer look shows a wry smile, an inner comment, perhaps, on the whole business of posing. The way in which she holds her head, long necklaces, the weight of a dark, plush coat — the impression is of confidence, solidity. The picture was taken in the early 1930s.

Last year, talking to Aunt Sonia on the telephone, I asked what happened to her grandmother, my great-grandmother. The solid woman of the photograph.

"She perished," said my aunt.

"Where? How?"

"She was killed by the Russians."

"By the Russians? When?"

"At the beginning of the war."

"In 1940? Were the Russians killing Jews in Poland? Wasn't it the Germans, the occupation in the east? Wouldn't it have been '41 or '42? Anyway, what *happened*?"

"She perished."

The next time I visited her, I asked Aunt Sonia to help me draw up a family tree. Herself at the centre. The others perched in branches above and around. The leaves of the tree fluttered in Austria, Poland, the Ukraine, and then across the world. An autumnal scattering. Ernestina, Theodora, Gershon. And here, the children, Maria, Leon, Chaim, Marie-Elizabeth. A diaspora of names, arranged in clusters. Gregor, Jacob, Miriam. And on the other side, Jakub, Szmul, Hillel. Now who was on my uncle's side, yes, Irena, Ludwik, Evgenie, Oskar, Mordechai. And their uncles and aunts, over here: Adam, Louisa, Joseph. The grandparents were Isaiah and Christina.

As she filled in the slots, Aunt Sonia muttered questions to herself. "Who *were* the Einbach children? The Zelkowicz parents? The Liebman grandparents?" At one point she said, as if reciting a line she had read in the Talmud, "The soul of the world is locked up in names."

I thought: I am asking Aunt Sonia to make a journey, albeit cryptic, to a history that seems not to be on her mind. And yet — how naive it would be to expect otherwise! — the names came pouring out. And with the names a ghastly conjugation. Bronislava, she perished.

Ludwik's brother, he perished. The sisters, they perished. She perished, he perished, they perished. I put a thin red line through the victims.

All family trees are a journey to the graveyard. Other families' naming would have been worse: many of my relatives escaped: leaves did fall in England, Canada, Australia and Israel. No, the weight of Aunt Sonia's story lay in the word "perished." These were not men and women and children who *died*. They did not end their lives in a particular year, or at a particular place, or as a result of particular diseases. No long illness, no sudden heart attack, no tragic accident. Nothing comic. No one run over by a tram. Not even a mysterious suicide. Nothing that let death affirm life. They "perished."

I looked at the names we had written. I pressed Aunt Sonia for details, asking her to recall what she knew of circumstances that might differentiate each one of our family within the amassed slaughter. She looked up from the white sheets of paper I had spread on her kitchen table and asked, "Can anyone bring a loved one to mind with only a memory of the eyes?"

"Isn't that one of the reasons for making a family tree," I said.

She replied: "Without a name I can't bring anyone to mind."

"And here are the names; you remember so many," I told her.

"I can bring them back to life," she said. "I can bring back their lives. But that's all. As for the deaths . . . "

She paused, then said: "I haven't heard, I never heard." She paused again. "I can't remember. Why don't you ask Cousin Elsa? She would know."

I wanted to know.

But for Aunt Sonia, I decided, the details of this family tree, the actual history, from the beginning of a name to its end, would be too terrible to endure. The bits and pieces of the tree that she marked out for me were a form of quick memory, a flicking on and off of lights. As a whole, the making of our family tree was a reference — detailed and personal — but only a reference to an episode. A madness. From which Aunt Sonia had, more or less, removed herself.

I did ask Cousin Elsa for details. Older than Aunt Sonia, and someone who fled east behind the retreating Russian lines, she knew far more. She recollected circumstances. Her child died of starvation in Lvov, 1940. Her husband died in Dachau in October 1943. Her brothers-in-law were shipped to Auschwitz in '44. Her favourite brother, a member of the Polish underground, was tortured to death. Also '44. Weeping, she said: "I should have died too." I stopped asking.

I had learned enough. I could tell my children, should they ever need to know, how their family came to England. More or less what happened to their grandparents, great uncles and aunts. I could tell them about Aunt Sonia. I could tell myself. It had been enough, almost, to spend time with Aunt Sonia, to listen to her, as I had those summers long ago, and to have seen her box of photographs.

I began wondering, what is the difference between knowing and not knowing the facts? Aunt Sonia knew that people were killed in their hundreds and hundreds of thousands. Among them individuals she loved; family members, who in part gave her her life, perished. So of course she knew. Yet I found myself thinking that she kept the knowledge generalized in order not to wish, day after day, like Cousin Elsa, that she too had died.

The night after my conversation with cousin Elsa I had a dream about Aunt Sonia. She had grown very tall and elegant, her hair was long and fair. She was walking down some unfamiliar boulevard, carrying a parasol. She stopped and turned to look at me. She said: "There must be some belief, some hope." I felt a sudden shame, as if the beam of her eye carried guilt deep into me. She seemed to wait for an answer, but none came. So she said: "One seeks to be more than a crippled survivor." Still I made no answer. She said: "The grief will be yours." The words seemed to wake me, already true in part.

The following weekend I went to see Aunt Sonia. I tried to be normal, attempted to gossip. But she was distracted. I asked her what was on her mind.

"I've been thinking about what happened. About the turning point," she said.

I felt uneasy, a moment of distant dread. As if she had anticipated questions I had decided never to ask.

"I left Vienna," she said. "I went to Paris. I believed that France was safe. I thought the Nazis would never take France."

She paused.

"I wasn't the only one. We heard that many German generals believed that the French army was too strong for their blitzkrieg. I shared the opinions of the German generals! But they were executed." Her voice became very quiet, she seemed so small in her neat cardigan and permed hair. "I had to run again. That was the turning point."

"In what way?"

"In what way! Europe had ended! Berlin, Vienna, Paris — all in the hands of the insane barbarians. All culture was finished."

"So you came to England." I had heard this part of the story many times before.

"I came to London, to wait. To see what was going to happen. To choose a place to go. Palestine? Australia? I wasn't sure. But definitely not here!"

She laughed and shrugged. Then she talked for a long time, in a quiet voice, without sadness or anger. Bit by bit she had settled in England in a rather English way. She felt safe. Protected. And in a Birmingham factory, where she was sent to work on a shoe-making machine, she met a shortsighted, unglamorous, movingly decent Englishman. They became lovers. He moved in with her. The wider protection of the nation had its echo in a narrow domestic safety.

When Aunt Sonia told me about the Birmingham man, it was to explain why she did not leave Europe. She laughed about the unlikely passion they felt for each other. She said, "I think he appreciated a bit of noise." Before the war ended — though at a time when its outcome was no longer in doubt — he left her. And married a neighbour. "Not young, not beautiful. But more suitable," she said. "Really I didn't mind." Then she started to spend time with our family — with its brand-new generation. The summer visiting had begun.

A few weeks after Aunt Sonia had told me about her journeys in the early years of the war, she talked about the immediate aftermath of the war. The period during which she learned who had survived. She suddenly said: "The names I knew were Heydrich and Eichmann and Himmler."

I said: "I suppose you mean you can't know the names of the men who really committed the murders."

She did not answer.

I sat there, at her kitchen table, imagining the names of the young men who flicked a whip, fired a revolver, tied a noose around a neck, managed the daily gassings. Grief was clutching at my stomach. I had nothing to say. But she broke the silence: "No names. No details. Specialists track some of them down. I am not a specialist."

The next day she sent me a postcard. On it was written a cryptic little message: "Heydrich, Eichmann, Himmler. Another family tree. The family of murder."

I imagined her as she wrote that, thinking: Our family tree is over here, with those that perished marked through with a thin red line. Their family tree is over there, with those who were said ultimately to be responsible for the murders marked in bold. No details surround the names of the dead; no details of the actual murderers either. Both family trees wrapped, smothered, in silence.

I thought: I must accept the silence. I feared the grief. But I wrote Aunt Sonia a reply to her card. I said: "Everywhere the small facts remain deeply hidden. There is an inevitability about the ignorance: in the midst of genocide, individual death is hard to isolate. What can we know of my great-grandmother's murder other than as one of a batch?" I did not tell her that I had begun to imagine, over and over, the moment when she was the one who climbed on the bodies in a pit, the moment when she became the next one to be shot. Images built from her photograph, and from an archive of old pictures. No colour. Nothing vivid. I began to know how difficult it was to get beyond her having simply perished. Aunt Sonia had turned the tables on me: I kept thinking we had talked about the family tree enough.

Aunt Sonia, however, surprised me.

I visited her a week or so after receiving her postcard and sending her my letter. She said she wanted to talk about why we had written to one another. I said: "Isn't there a problem of circumstances? I mean, if a member of a family is assaulted or killed, other members — the survivors — memorialize the wound and grief by knowing as much as can be known. The name of a rapist or a murderer, the details of a punishment." She listened with unusual attention, murmuring once: "They are buried under heaps of bodies."

I went on. "The trouble is, we are cut off from both the crime and the criminal. Between those that 'perished' and the gross figures of Heydrich, Eichmann, Himmler, there is little more than a sense of some foul gang. They had power, then were defeated. Of course we know that members of the gang survived and scattered about the world, ageing in hiding. Odd ones are winkled out and dragged into the light. Then we are given the personal stories we need. But these stories do not establish for sure that this or that one killed in such and such a manner on an actual day some particular relative. These stories at the trials, or even those in the detailed work that comes from searching archives, offer nothing that can be marked beside the red lines on the family tree."

I looked at her, thinking I wanted to stop these thoughts. I said: "Is that what you meant by your postcard? On our tree the labels without settings, and on the other side the selected names in bold."

I had finished, or, more likely, had puzzled myself to a long pause. She said: "I don't think so. No. I don't think that is so."

I said: "So what do you mean? Or is it all too horrible to talk of any more?"

She looked at me and smiled. "I don't know. Now I am tired."

The attempt at the family tree, the repetitions of the word "perish," the thoughts and conversations between us that followed, some coincidence of things, the moment in our modern histories, whatever there was, for both of us, in the air — for some such set of reasons Aunt Sonia began to do research.

At first it was a bit of a book here, a bit of a book there. Quite soon she was a devoted — dare I say "fanatical"? — extramural graduate student of the holocaust.

The first phone call came on a Sunday evening. I remember I was in the middle of getting the children to bed. I had begun telling the latest story about giants and mountains. I picked up the phone, eager only to get off it again. When I heard Aunt Sonia's voice I suppose I resigned myself to the weekend news update. But she had a different kind of news on her mind. Her voice was slow; without its usual quickfire qualities, without its energetic confidence. She sounded measured, didactic:

"I've been reading. Listen. In Hungary they didn't begin the killing until 1944. Did you know that?"

"No."

"Not until the war was as good as over. But that's not the point. The point is, the Hungarian police did it. I mean, 2,000 local police pushed them all into the trains." Still her voice paced out each fact, step by step. "They counted them, 75 to a car, and drove them in with whips. Seventy-five to a car. Old people were dying right there at the station. The police forced them in. It took 65 days to send 400,000 to be gassed. The murderers. The police were murderers."

She said more. She restated this discovery, measured it out in different ways as if to be sure, as if to be able to present this history with neither doubt nor embellishment. In each part, from each angle, she always ended with the police. *They* surprised her.

The next call came a couple of days later. At Tuesday lunch time. Not a moment she would usually phone me. Again the slow voice. I thought: is she a little drunk? My attempt, no doubt, at a first line of defence.

"I've read something else. There were over 50,000 concentration camp and slave labour guards at their posts at the end of the war. Fifty thousand! Who were they all?"

Then on Wednesday night:

"Romania was one of the worst. I've discovered that Himmler complained that the Romanians were being too efficient. Twice. Two different complaints. The German camps couldn't cope with the number of people they were sending to be slaves or killed. That was in 1941, and I think in '42."

Friday:

"Heydrich had a plan. All worked out. And he thought people all over Europe would help him. And lists. In January 1942 — just before he was blown up — he showed all his lists. He even had marked out 300,000 in England. These were the people he expected to be exterminated here."

I said that I was not surprised that there were plans and lists. The Germans are famous for efficiency. This exasperated her.

"No, no. That's not it. They didn't just have plans. They had an expectation. They were sure that they would be helped. That there would be *co-operation*."

The phone kept ringing. Over the coming weeks Aunt Sonia passed on the facts she could not bear to keep to herself. The details she could not live with. The discoveries that ate at the foundation of her hopes. I heard about the Ukraine, Poland, France, Greece, Czechoslovakia, Holland, Norway . . . I became used to her new, strange way of talking to me. I was drawn into the rhythm of her calculations.

The research, like the voice, was relentless — and had its pattern: Aunt Sonia was mapping out the spread of that other family tree. She was marking innumerable, innumerable dots, and then joining them together. From trunk to branch to twigs to leaves. From Lithuanian guards to German gas-chamber manufacturers, to businessmen with slave labourers on their production lines, to mechanics who fixed death truck exhausts, to Latvians who assisted the murder squads, to Poles who extracted teeth from corpses, to railway workers, to researchers into the useful poisons.

Aunt Sonia, marking and joining these dotlike facts, was drawing a baobab of immense proportions. Limbs of this huge tree reached the width and breadth of the Europe the Germans managed to dominate. Branches spread through civil service offices, police stations, nationalist political organizations, churches. Its leaves fluttered down in quiet backyards, seemingly harmless living rooms, and on homes in every town and village of the war zones and occupied lands.

The last of the history phone calls was the most troubled and the longest. Her voice had now lost its measured tones. She spoke much faster, yet without restatements, no emphatic or balancing repetition. At the beginning of this call she tried to tell me something about Italy and Bulgaria — the countries to which, apparently, the arms of the monstrous tree did not quite reach. A reprieve. I clutched at the reprieve. Encouraged it. I said: "Ordinary people were on every side. For and against. The Resistance. Socialists as well as prison guards. Attempts on Hitler's life. Men and women in every country who risked everything to save Jews."

But she changed tack altogether and said, "I don't suppose you know about Evian."

"Evian?"

"The conference. They talked about refugees."

"Who talked about them?"

"Everyone. England. America. Australia. Mexico. And others."

She told me that this was the beginning of restrictions. At the very moment of despairing need, they restricted immigration.

"They shut them in," she said. "They turned groups back at the Swiss border. Do you know why? Can you imagine such a thing? Because the Swiss government, in its wisdom, ruled that racial discrimination was not a good enough reason to be a refugee. Not a good enough reason!"

She hesitated. Then shouted down the phone at me: "Are you still there?"

"Yes."

"I thought you'd gone. I'll tell you. Even Finland, even the one country whose rulers defied the extermination plans, even the country where they said 'kill us first if you plan to kill our people.' Even from Finland fifty Austrian refugees were sent back to Austria, back to the Germans. Why? Because their visas were not 'in order,' because they came from the Austrians and not from the Finns."

"I didn't know."

"Of course you didn't. So I'm telling you. You have to know. And something else. Do you know something else?" She didn't wait for my answer. "I've discovered about the Americans. Thousands of Jews could have escaped, would have been allowed out, if there had been boats to carry them. The Americans said they could not provide boats. No ships available." Her voice was getting louder: "They said there weren't any boats — and at the same time they were shipping tens of thousands of German prisoners of war! And not just the Americans. The British too. They refused to let children escape. And something else. There were deals with the Nazis that would have saved thousands more. Yes." She shouted. "Eichmann offered lives for gold! But the deals fell through: the British and Americans created currency and shipping difficulties. Always difficulties. Delays. No deals were possible. A million could have been saved." She shrieked at me, in a sort of climax for her facts: "They were condemned to death, by our allies. And do you know? They wouldn't bomb the railway lines to Auschwitz. They said there were technical reasons. They let the trains keep running!" And after this scream, she said quietly, "That was the 400,000 Hungarians. The ones the police had loaded." Then her voice faltered. I realized that she was at a loss. And, lost, she asked about the children.

Aunt Sonia never mentioned her research again. But she did not return to any ordinary way of talking. In fact, she could no longer stop herself from talking. She had always been a chatterbox. But now, in her endless stream of words, now she was compulsive, frantic. Words like small bricks with which she built a high, thick wall. It was infuriating. Then alarming. She alienated everyone. She appeared to be self-obsessed, drowning in her own trivia. So noisy. And so inconsequential.

Then, suddenly, "elle se tut." I borrow the use of the expression from a French short story I once read. And I think her end is best expressed in French. "Elle se tut." She shut up. I was told by her doctor— an old family friend — that it could have been an overdose. Perhaps, just possibly, an accident. Who knows?

Her silence, at first, was the silence of the world. All around and within me. I went to her house. I stood in the kitchen, in order to remember her. Her absence, like all the absences of the dead to whom we stand adjacent, if only for moments, was like a blanket over the soul, a brief suffocation. In grief we close our eyes, we gasp, we gulp for air. We try and muster the facts.

I stood in her kitchen; and when I breathed again and opened my eyes, I asked myself: why did she choose silence? Something to do, I was sure, with the roots of the spreading tree. Where did these roots find their sustenance? What social compost, what system of society made this tree take its shape and then grow with such relentlessness? Until its deformity became the norm, its leaves the colour of every time of year.

I thought: here is the unbearable discovery. For she had to continue, had no choice but to continue, to live on the earth where this tree had its roots. No possible land existed without the hummocks and furrows of its system. The soil of its nurture — the earth of Europe — has not been, can not be, remade or replaced. Its leaves lie skeletal everywhere. Cut off stumps and old branches are the framework of our way of life. Both trees — our family of labels and the latticework of murderers — occupy a one and only terrain. There could be no more innocence. With her new facts, Aunt Sonia could no longer have hope.

She left me a letter. I don't think of it as a suicide note. We had often written to each other. But this was strange, a surprise. It was like a work of scholarship. Quotes were linked by questions. The quotes came

from letters I had written to her. The questions were hers. This strange
document reached me after "elle se tut," after the silence. As I read the
quotes and questions I felt that, even after all these years, I was still the
little boy sitting on the Persian rug in the spare bedroom of our family
home, being told that I must continue to be her representative. It was
the last of our conversations.

In quoting Aunt Sonia's final letter, I realize I am quoting quotes and
paraphrases of myself. A curious turning inward of the circle. A resolve,
on Aunt Sonia's part, to carry the issue forward — if only into another
generation. She may have been offering me the escape that had, after
more than half a century of trying, failed her. In this letter she said:

. . . You wrote to me on May 8th, 1972. You told me about your first
trip to the Arctic. You said: "I looked down from the windows of a Twin
Otter aeroplane. We were circling the settlement, beginning to land.
We had flown for nearly two hours. Over nothing but nothing. Tundra
and then the ice of Hudson Bay. No fields. No walls. No *property.* And
the ice, both of the lakes and the sea, is every shade of blue and green.
This supposed emptiness is full of unbelievable beauty."

She followed this with the question: Is emptiness what you needed?
And went on: I don't think so.

You wrote in July: "The tundra is marked by such subtleties. Of
plants that thread themselves into the permafrost and tuck themselves
into the shelter of rocks and tussocks, and whose flowers are small and
delicate and vivid with a miniature brilliance. And the subtlety of the
tracks of animals — lemming trails worn into the earth, weasel and fox
prints across a snowbank. And above all, or subtlest of all in the human
scheme of things, signs of people. Graves and cairns and tent rings and
the remains of an old turf and bone house. These are everywhere yet
make no difference to the surface of this world. Layer upon layer of
men and women whose remains are solid, made of stone and bone and

shaped wood, and at the same time ghostly, delicate, integral to the landscape."

She wrote after this: Were ghosts what you needed?

I think not. I remember you told me that the people of the north have avoided — what did you call it? — the neolithic catastrophe. You meant, I think, that when there was no agriculture, when human beings were hunters, they had a way of life in which men and women acknowledged their dependence on one another and therefore were equal. That there was no ownership of the things people needed in order to live. No private lands. No private fishing. That they did not tyrannize children. Nor tyrannize themselves with worries about their children. You wrote in a letter, in January 1980:

"This is a world without fields. I look across from where I live, and see land. Resources, not development. I travel with hunters. They are individualists, but there is no competition. They harvest, but with no sense that their taking will leave less for others — or that their failure could come from others' success."

And Aunt Sonia asked: Is there, after all, a system beyond mass murder? Have you travelled to where there is, or was, or can be envisaged, a redemption? You said only a year ago, in a springtime letter: "The men and women of this camp sit and wait. They appear to sift the world around them without anxiety, as if thinking were no more anxious, no more hesitant, than drinking tea. They are waiting for the wind to change direction, the animals to move further to the north, the children to feel well, for things to be *right*. They are calculating without the paraphernalia of outward rationality; they are intuiting without self-conscious insistence on intuition. In a fully human way, they think. So with calm, they wait."

The final line of this letter was her question: "What did you think they were waiting for?"

EVA

They have given me a dark room. Better to know God in a small space. I look up at a window, to the sky. There is no horizon.

I pray to you, God, up there in your heaven, beyond the light.

As a child I bared myself to you. How I sighed in my prayers. With what engulfing weeping I sent myself towards you. Out into the light. O Lord who hast given us creation, for whom all things are the fruit! I offered my childish faith, morning and evening, on my knees by a bed, my face squeezed into my hands, the tears pressed back into moist eyes. Morning and evening, in paroxysms of faith.

Where otherwise might I find eternity, a blending of myself with another, a consummation? From loneliness I cried out to you. With all the solitude of the human condition. At six or seven or eight years old, at all my childhood ages, I knew that with your being I could at last be fused. One with another. With *the* other. No longer by myself in this aching, bony form. No longer marooned with hands and flesh, hands consoling flesh. No longer a child by himself. No longer without a centre, with no right to exist. So much, so absolutely everything, can come from you.

O God, I do not now pray for my release. As you look into my mind's eye, you will see — as I see — the etchings of another landscape, faint lines on that glass wall between me and you, between me and everything. As you decipher, as you must, the meanings of these lines, as you recognize the wide territory carved on my soul, as you see the figures on the sea ice, against the grey and green tundra, in the vast sunlight, forgive me. But do not let me out of this incarceration, this dark and tight little space, this horizonless world. Keep me here to suffer the damnation I have earned. At least until the glass wall with its stubborn etchings is shattered. Destroy me, God, by keeping me alive. Amen.

Before I had heard of missions and missionaries I longed for a journey. Even a small child has the image if not the words to feel the innocent longing to make good our possibilities by travel.

The first short expedition: a tour of the missionary centre. With you, the very reverend, the utterly fatherly, the allseeing Dr Paulus, the man of such age and substance and speaking such elegant English — a first surprise in this Germany. "We must speak English," you said. "This may be the place, these are not the times, for German." My first lesson, my first exercise, the cold rich language of the new empires.

He praised me. Encouraged. Urged. And pointed to those grey images on the walls of the corridors. "The *Harmony*," he said, "our ship. She sails each summer to the northern stations." Stations? "Our villages," he said, and laughed, and told me about the clumps of rhubarb and delphinium flowering against wild shacks. He gestured at a group of faces smiling out of their furs. He told me names. Atagutaluk. Kusugak. He showed me pictures of the forest, the tundra behind, the rocks of the coast, even birds — gannets, I think, suspended in clear arctic sky. I stared at each image, aching to be there, up there, now . . .

This year, I said. I can go this year? He said, in his slow, quizzical manner, "Are you ready?" Ready, yes, with the faith to escape, the knowledge that only somewhere far . . . Reverend Paulus, with his English voice and grandfatherly face, he marked the first lines, helped begin the etchings, on the glass walls that divide me from . . . from everything.

And he said, "I shall be returning on *Harmony*'s next voyage. My furlough is ended. We would be companions in adventure!" But his adventure was long matured, balanced, contemplated, contained by his clarity of purpose, protected by well-established comforts. With his duty, his family, and God in his own small corner. Balanced and orderly and pale. He took me into his wide study, sat me on his leather chairs, showed me his old manuscripts, guided me into the steps of the missionary endeavour, educated me in geography and history, always with his quiet voice, always seeking to balance, even to restrict. I looked at him, looked up to him, seeing through his quiet to the roar of northern oceans (though he said, "The sea, for the most part, is calm; we stay in the shelter of the fjords and bays"); to the flash of electric storms in the midsummer nights (despite his informing me that "Thunder and lightning are unknown, to all intents and purposes, along the Labrador coast"); to the conversion of savage minds into Christian purity (did I hear him tell me that "Our people, you know, are all Christians of a rough and tumble kind"?). Yes, he tried to check and balance, to effect the appropriate disappointments long before we set sail. And the outcome of our conversations: an inflaming of every nerve's excitement.

Did my reverend father, my model of rational moderation, begin this madness in me? He comes to my mind's eye with the ease of an obsession. Yet he is a part, not a cause, of my imprisonment.

The walls of this room are brown. Like a library that has lost its books. A place to read with neither words nor illumination.

I knew, I always have known, that God would come clad in the costume of the least of us. How shall I recognize you then? Ready as I am to be taken into and held by whatever costume, be it the shabbiest, the least or most hirsute of bodies. I had always feared, still fear, a mistake, a failure of recognition, a confusion of identity. How can I know you? Before, during all this, I feared.

Is there forgiveness?

No prayer should end with a question. The Almighty's grip on circumstances is unsure. We in our prisons down here must tell him, over and over, how things are. Heaven requires its affirmations. For thine is the kingdom, and the power . . .

When did the evil begin?

In the dressing room. At the theatre — the pride of a hidden German town. Only a provincial little place, with a dressing room that Eva shared. I forget now who with. I remember the mirror, the desk light among a clutter of colours and combs and frills. Eva was sitting there, dressing, undressing. How had I dared to enter this forbidden domain? I had watched her sing. The voice had swarmed into every part of me. The voice of the angels, of the centre of the universe, of the clouds, of love without question, of death's inevitability. There are no words for the power of a voice in music. I had gone round to the stage door, walked through as if I were an actor, muttered to the doorman, "guten Abend, guten Abend," found her name on a door. And knocked.

We were lovers, Eva and I. We had pledged our souls. We had touched hands. We had felt the shock in one another's beings. I had knelt before her. And we had spoken, in English, in German.

We had never kissed.

I knocked on the dressing room door, and she called out, "Who is it?" "Me, Heinrich." "Come in." As I opened the door I saw her reflection in the mirror. Her eyes were closed. She was alone. I was carrying flowers — a bunch of roses. How had I got them? From a salesgirl in the theatre foyer? At the stage door? I handed them to her. But she didn't see. I looked from her closed eyes to where she sat. She was immobile, hands reaching round to her back. She was holding a zip or a fastener. Her shoulders were bare. I was confused, embarrassed. I looked away, then back again. She spoke my name. "Heinrich. Heinrich." I moved towards her, to the table to set down the flowers, to the bare shoulders to touch the skin. "Eva."

Her eyes still closed, she began to hum. Soft, slow humming. The music of the performance.

I put my hands on her shoulders. I knelt — rather, fell to my knees — behind her. My arms on her back. My face between my arms. In prayer.

Somehow she turned. Somehow the costume had fallen loose; she had moved her hands, had let go the fastener. She was naked. This woman, my Eva, whom I had never touched, was naked. One of my arms reached up, to her mouth, her eyes. The other lay on her body. My face, between my arms, was between her breasts. She pulled me into her, into softness, into safety. With her hands on the back of my head she gave me permission. My mouth, my lips felt the nakedness. Permission for us to be one with another. I imagine that she opened her eyes. Mine were closed. She said: "It is good to wait."

I said: "Du bist mir Alles. You are everything to me."

She said: "In a year we will be married."

She took my head and moved it so I rested on one breast, then the other. Then she raised my mouth to hers. She said: "Du bist mir Alles."

How simple to recall that evening, the moment of first and unreal consummation. The original blasphemy. The substitution of Eva for God. Because that *is* what you would say about it, isn't it? No, I'm not talking to God now. I'm talking to you, Father, you my moral mentor, my superior. How you quizzed me in that large study, that book-lined library of a room, with views all around of intelligence.

— "Are you sure that she is suitable? Marriage is any life's most *serious* undertaking."

How curious that you emphasized the word "serious," as if its meaning did not suffice unto the task. As if you were intent on conveying some bitter little irony.

— "For you, dear Heinrich, for all of us Moravians, perhaps for all truly Christian missionaries, it is doubly, triply so. Serious and difficult."

Would there be especial difficulty, I wondered. Because I was to be a missionary? Or because we are Moravians, *real* Christians. Unlike, I supposed, the Oblates — but they would not have the problem of marriage! Or was I to understand that my first marriage was to Christ, and second to a mortal body? Perhaps the isolation, the Arctic... What could you have had in mind just then? Did you already feel the beginnings of a blasphemy?

— "She is English. I appreciate that benefit. Our missions must be English. German is already, how shall I say it? An awkwardness. English is the language of the new century and of the new world, as it is the language of trade. You would learn to live a married life in English. Which we would welcome. But is she practical? Reliable? She is, is she not, a singer? An artist, would you say?"

I said nothing. Except: I couldn't live anywhere without her.

— "The station is not merely anywhere. It is, in a certain sense, nowhere. Nowhere you can *know*. A place one can scarcely imagine."

I said that I was sure we, Eva and I, had God's blessing. A conjunction made in heaven.

— "The blessings of God may be easier to know than those of our fellow man. Or woman."

I told him: she is deeply religious.

— "You will be separated for a year. You will be alone there. You will have much to learn. Wives — or wives to be — travel on the boat of the next summer, when the ice has gone."

He paused. His eyes stared at me. His face was lined and hairy: eyebrows, beard, moustache — all protuberant and dense. A clear, cold man. A superior in our Church.

— "You understand, Heinrich, that Moravians approve, must approve the brides of our young missionaries. The choice, after all, is both personal and collective. A matter of taste and discipline. As marriage should be. A mixture of elements. Your heart and your duty; your self and your society."

I understood, Reverend Father. I understood that I would go alone to the north, and that after one year, when the mission boat returned, it would bring to me my Eva. A year. Both a long and brief period. An interval. A time for readiness. She had said we must wait. We would. We could. Dear God, you must believe that I did believe that we could.

I waited for the journey to the north. To the place where I would begin, and begin, also, to wait — the preparing for my Eva. Making a nest — and, Paulus would have said, the denial of the flesh. And yet there was none, neither flesh nor denial. Instead, a heating of the body by its most feared hopes. I did not seize my member and yearn. I rolled in a bed, but with a passion for leaving, waiting. We had fused already. The community of two had been made — or so I believed, most completely and darkly believed.

The day came when I loaded my trunk onto the deck of the *Harmony*. The brass lock and clasps shone. A leather strap wound around my possessions, my new needs. The ship's boys hauled it below, stowed it away in the cabin for novitiates. The panelling of my cabin reeked of wax and polish.

Eva was with me. She climbed up onto the highest deck, and together we stared out at the estuary of the Elbe, towards the Hamburg docks, to the flat and cluttered land beyond, out to the river again, towards where the sea must begin. We clung to each other. We gazed into one another. We said nothing. We embraced. Whistles blew. The harbour pilot came on board. Men gathered at the winches and by the ropes for the topsail and jib. We clung to each other, then parted.

I watched Eva step by step down the *Harmony*'s ladder and onto the quayside. She stopped there, frozen, pale, a hand on her heart. Our eyes met for a last farewell. Whistles blew. The anchors were hauled, the ropes cast off from the shore. The pilot shouted orders. Ropes threshed and whined in their pulleys. Sails lifted. The *Harmony* rolled into the Elbe, out towards Helgolander Bucht, the Nordsee, the first shock of the open sea.

What did I feel? Dementia? Terror? The beginnings of seasickness? Love? Everything at once, I suppose, in the chaos of this great and terrible moment.

I climbed down to my cabin, to my trunk with its leather belt. To my new needs. I lay on my bunk, and slept. You woke me, Father. Your eyes bright on mine, your hand so strong on my shoulder, shaking me. "We are at sea, Heinrich. At sea." And I heard the rigging moan and the ship's boards creak. And I felt the rhythm of a boat powered by full sail, thrusting before the wind. "We are going back, Heinrich, back at last!" Ah yes, Father, you were returning from your furlough. Returning with your acolyte in tow. Behind whom, in the foams and ripples of the wake, splashed my image of Eva, hand on breast, eyes on mine, beginning her year-long vigil.

The darkness of this room is no comfort, nor does it help carry to me my memories. At times they attach me to the hard little bed in here. They say I am dangerous, that my lack of faith streams out of the corners of my mouth. That I am a savage in my attachments to another realm. That I leap at the edges of this room and smash my head against whatever could be hard enough to split me open and let me out. I imagine that they sit, those doctors of the Moravian persuasion, those men who will save both body and soul, in their consulting room and worry that I am possessed by a devil. For this must be Satan's work. Strapped into myself. Strait jacketed. And the figures etched still on the glass wall within me, cutting me off.

Do I rave in English or German? The figures on the glass speak an altogether different language.

I no longer remember more than the mists of the journey north. I have forgotten what I saw as we crossed the Atlantic. Nor even as we made a way up the Newfoundland coast. I suppose there were icebergs and fog and offloadings at villages along the way.

But I do remember a dream. The second, perhaps the third night of that journey north, one night at the end of a day I had lain half-awake and nauseous in my cabin. Paulus had visited me with broth and consolations. I dreamed of Eva.

She was as I saw her at the theatre, in the dressing room. Sitting with her back to me. The room was full of her music. And the back was bare as it had been then. But now she sat high, on a tall stool, a modelling chair. High above me. And she turned towards me, as she had when we declared the infinity of our love, naked. Large and naked and above me. She leaned forwards. She smiled into my eyes. The sound of her singing continued, as if she were an opera ventriloquist, coming not from her mouth but echoing from deep within in her and throughout the space around her. I reached up to her. She reached down and caught my hands in hers. She turned my palms upwards, towards her — her hands on the backs of mine, controlling them, taking charge of all their movements. She looked at my hands, at my eyes. She lifted my hands a little higher.

She said: "I can be in love with you." She said: "But you must accept my price."

Your price? Is there a bargain? "The oldest of bargains, between a woman and a man."

And the payment? "I shall be in love with you. You must love me above everything. My love for yours. Agreed? Agreed."

She lifted my hands to her, laying them on her, pressing them into her. And now I heard her song, the echoes from inside her being. A soft, insinuating song.

I screamed. I tore my hands from her. I shouted above the sounds of the music — neither my shouts nor the words of the song had any meaning.

And I woke. As from a nightmare. I was upright in my narrow bunk, moist with sweat, muttering "Nein, nein, so müss es nicht sein! No, it mustn't be thus!" I could hear the sea as our mission boat rolled against its force. I pulled on boots and threw my outer cloak over my shoulders and climbed onto the deck. A blind darkness was made of spray and rain. Somewhere beyond the invisible was a shoreline, and far away to the west and north the forests of a remote interior. I stared out to where they must have been, trying to look to the future. But the dream held me. Was it so hard, then, to leave my Eva? To travel ahead of her, to prepare a way for her to follow towards the destiny in which, at last, we would join? In the darkness, from the unseen shore, I imagined I could hear her voice: "Du bist mir Alles. So bist du mein Alles."

Lost to recollection are my first steps ashore at Okkak, the mission station where Paulus and I and our supplies were offloaded. No doubt the people gathered around and stared: in these places, the *Harmony*'s arrival heralded the centre of time — the end of one year, the beginning of another. Furs would be taken out; provisions brought in. Journeys begun and ended. This was the fulcrum of the seasons, the means for effecting all real change. Despite this importance, it is not in my mind. Derangement has clouded the missionary centre.

Instead in the nostrils of memory I can smell the air, taste its sharp cold and the tangs carried in it of seal oil and unwashed bodies and dogs. And wood smoke. And horizons. I imagine I can feel horizons in my breath.

They installed me in one of the wooden frame and plank houses built so square in the German style. They gave me food. They took me to the church. I listened to the brass band play German and English hymn tunes. And Dr Paulus. The man who had the task of learning the secrets of my soul in order to be sure that I acclimatized in an appropriate manner. Dr Paulus, tall and thin and sixty — only now, in a landscape, in work, that called out for extraordinary strength, did I notice his build and age. Paulus, my overseer, trainer and father confessor. He it was who told me that I must begin with the language, Inuttut. "It means" he said, "the way that the Eskimo do things." He also said, "Learn that and you will learn everything."

Can those have been his words? If so, he could not have meant them. He brought me not to God's but to Satan's project. From the beginning there is another face, another pair of dark eyes, another body. Ulayuk. Who dives in the snow. And who watches white men with eyes full of speculation. Who like all of us longs for warmth. "Ulayuk," said Dr Paulus, "will teach you the language."

He brought me to her, that we — Ulayuk and I — might get to know each other.

— "Take me into your house."

I told her it was not allowed. That only the missionaries could go inside.

— "Teach me English."

I said that I knew very little, that if I taught anything it would be German, that I now must learn *her* language.

— "We can teach one another."

Summer ended. New ice edged its way around our shorelines. I crouched inside. Dr Paulus took me into his world — of duties and trade. How a man must know and honour the path he is on. How I should understand the value of an immature white fox. The perfectibility of the human soul. The slyness of the Eskimo hunter clinging, as he put it, to his drums and his dreams. How he talked!

And he took me outside, for what he called our practicals. We watched the trappers unwrap and sort their furs. We watched them brew tea on the beach and joke among themselves. We stood close to them. And we watched them leave again for somewhere that Paulus termed "mere distance." We stood side by side in the air and breathed.

Our practicals in the open were brief. Dr Paulus felt the cold. But there was always something to be remarked upon. In particular we watched the dog teams setting out onto the ice. Once, when the new ice had formed, we stood in a chill half-light and saw line after line of dogs and sleds — nine or ten of them — move away like a dark and fractured snake humped and twisting black on white. We watched for a long time — much longer than Dr Paulus usually could endure the cold. He broke a silence between us, saying: "They must come to us. To *our* encampment. To *our* God."

How Dr Paulus circled me with his notions, binding me to him as if I were his one and only child. I came to love the man. And he pitied me.

Once he asked: "In what measure do you love your Eva?"

I said, in every measure. How full of love we were! Dr Paulus said, "You must concentrate on your studies of the Eskimo language. You must go out into the people's camps. You must know them." Yes, Dr Paulus, you foresaw, didn't you, the coming struggle for God's children. I must understand them so that no one else could steal their loyalties — neither their souls nor their white foxes. I must understand them and bring them to us. To the path we were on. Ulayuk's path.

I walked, as you urged, along the winter shorelines. I set my face into the wind, and bowed my head against the blowing snow. I crouched outside. And then, on a frozen beach, I heard for the first time — not the voice of God calling me as he should, not the urging of the angels, but the sound of Eva singing. She sang to me from the other side of the cold sea. Over the new ice. Through the wind. Stronger and wilder than the wind. Shrieking at me. Frenzied arias. Crescendos of sound that burst onto my being. Eva, your songs reached me and tore me open.

The first time I heard the voice I ran to the mission building. I ran to Dr Paulus. Help me! Help me! She is calling, shrieking in song! But your study blocked out all such sounds. The singing stopped. And the next day you arranged for me to go out to the hunters' camps. Out to begin my lessons.

Between me and the dark walls of my cell are those first images of vastness. In the thudding of sledge runners on ridges of sea ice; in the hiss of dogs taking us through a surface of wind-blown snow; in the calling and laughter of the hunters; in the gentle bitterness of the air; in the distance that spread everywhere with pale eternity; in everything beyond the village and the mission building, the only voice calling to me was that of an all-embracing God. I passed into the world both clear and mysterious. My love for Eva passed easily into duty remembered, obligation undertaken. The etchings on the glass wall, the shapes of my madness, do not come from her or Dr Paulus or a mission station. They are the outline of a dog team, a thread of tracks on the snow, the long band of a floe edge between ice and sky, a dark line of immense horizon.

Ulayuk took me into her father's snowhouse. I was given a place of honour on a sleeping platform. Offered food and drink. And I fell asleep. To strange sounds, new voices. Another music. I can hear them, I can hear them! "Aukatugulalungani. Tanna qadlunaarapik uingatuapiutsuni surqaimat." The words came from the very front and the very depths of the mouth; guttural yet full of breath and lightness; and with a quiet force. No wonder this was a language whose speakers never interrupted one another! "Sungiutigiguniuk takananginirqsaulaarmijuq." At the beginning they had no meaning. Jumbles of sounds. On and on the murmuring voices.

The days of the camp followed one another. Piece by piece I assembled the jigsaw of Ulayuk's family's life. Or a picture, rather, of that life in which I could have some part. Fathers and mothers. Children. Faces that first stared, then smiled, then welcomed me.

I was taken to open water and shown how to lie in wait for harp seals that were now moving south in great herds. I was taken to breathing holes in the sea ice and left waiting for ringed seals to surface at my feet. I was shown lakes where I could dangle an ivory lure through a hole cut through the fresh-water ice.

No one expected me to succeed in hitting the bobbing head of a harp seal in the open water, or in thrusting a harpoon down into a ring seal's fat round body, or in impaling on the prongs of a leister the trout and char that darted in to examine my ivory lure. When I tried and failed, Ulayuk's family applauded and laughed.

At first I lived and hunted in the clothes provided by the mission: felt liners in sealskin boots, woollen trousers and cardigans, canvas outer clothing and oilskins, wool gloves covered in sailcloth. The Inuit appeared to admire these garments. But as winter set in, Ulayuk — along with the other women of our encampments — began to sew.

Caribou hides were turned into fur suits. And one was prepared for me.
The day came when I was summoned to one of the snowhouses and
dressed. Ulayuk said, "Take off all, just the caribou now." Incredulous,
I said the caribou must go on top of my wool and canvas and felt. They
cried out: "Aukka, aukka. No, no." And laughing, they urged me to
strip and then pull onto my bare skin the new garments with the fur
innermost. I was sheathed in caribou. And then, before setting out
onto the sea ice, I was shown how to pull another layer over the first,
this time the fur outermost. I became a bundle of caribou. No buttons
or zips; the trousers held up by a sinew twine; everything else pulled
on like a set of socks; until my head poked out through a furry opening;
and there even was a hood that I could pull over me, closing myself
finally into my body's own warmth.

In this wild outfit I tremulously ventured for the first time into the
winter's cold. The people laughed at me, yet made as if to admire the
quality of the skins, the perfection of the seams, the excellence of
Ulayuk's needlework. Within an hour I realized I now felt a warmth
that I had never known — as if, at last, I had found real comfort.

Dressed in my furs, I did, one afternoon in a winter sunless light,
plunge a harpoon head into a seal's shoulder, and found myself
struggling to drag the animal out of the sea onto the ice. And then my
little achievement, with all its confusion and panic, was celebrated as
if I had conquered a week's starvation. The meat of that young seal was
savoured as the rarest delicacy. Its hide scraped and stretched and
presented to me as captured gold.

And that night, after I had killed the seal and hauled it across the ice
to our camp, Ulayuk set her body against mine. Under the caribou
hides that were our bedding; she was naked. God knows I did not make
love with her. There was but darkness. We did not kiss. My head

between my arms. As in the Bible, according to its model of holy copulations, we lay together. In the darkness. Blinded by darkness. She took me into her. For ever.

And the voices, whose sense I had begun to understand: "Iliniar-galuarllunga — even though I learn." "Pijumallungalluni — and while I do want this." "Inungumarijjaiunirpunga — I shall never really be one of the people." "Aa taimangatau — yes, that's always the way." The murmuring voices. "Aa. Taimangatau."

All winter I lived in the snowhouses of the people. Slowly their sounds entered my throat, and the words — so many words — filled my brain. Where were you Eva? Where was your round beauty, your soft breasts? Never forgotten. I was always in shame. But the light and air exploded inside me. The horizons bewitched me. The rich, strange smells of animal fats and putrefying skins; of hunters' breath . . . and the darkness of the sleeping platform . . . Ulayuk's skin, which I never caressed but into whom, again and again, I slipped my way . . . All this engulfed me.

We celebrate the birth of Christ. They bring us to food, to music, and to pray. God, I do not ask for my release. Not yet. When the divide is opened, when I steer a way through. When . . . when . . . There is a tree, with candles. I kneel at the tree, pressing into my eyes. On Christmas morning the baby is born. There are visits. Eva does not come.

At the mission there was Christmas. The hunters came in to trade. In our camp in the snow there was one piece of Christmas magic: with neither calendars nor messengers from the Moravians, Ulayuk and her family knew that it was Christmas. Ulayuk said, "It is good for us to be close to the mission. For trade." One morning the sledges were loaded; we were moving. I supposed that it was time for a fresh snowhouse — the walls of our home were thick with ice and black with soot. Or that the hunters had resolved to move to better sealing grounds — for some days we had all stood too long beside breathing holes. Meat was running low. There would be insufficient fat for lamps. As everyone hurried back and forth between snowhouse and sledges, piling skins and boxes and clothing, I asked where we would be going.

"Kuviasukvingulirmat," they said. "It's happiness time. Bring your things here." Bewildered, I brought my things. Ulayuk could see that I did not understand. I said, "What is happening?" "Christmas," she said. "We will trade and have a party. We call it Kuviasukvik, a place for being happy."

Christmas? And the Reverend Father Paulus, he would be expecting me. He would be waiting for me, to resume our conversations. The sledges pulled away. The ice was smooth, the air still and sunlit. Ulayuk's father said: "Uvannik piqatiqarsivutit. You and me are going to be travelling companions."

He murmured "Hah," the call to the dogs to move. Our sledge lurched forwards; I was running to keep up. He cracked his immense whip around the dogs' ears: they went faster. I clutched at the thongs that tied our great bundle of possessions onto the wooden slats of the sledge, slipped, was pulled to the ice, was dragged for a moment alongside, then managed to jump onto the load. Ulayuk's father jumped beside me, and laughed.

I gulped the air, its cold biting at my windpipe, chilling down into my lungs. I looked around. Behind us three more teams of dogs raced their sledges towards us, eager to catch up, the men shouting and waving their whips. The beginning of Christmas!

We travelled for three days, making a snowhouse each evening. Sometimes we sat on the sledge as it creaked heavily over the good ice. When the ice was not good, when jagged lumps of frozen storm cluttered our route, we pushed and hauled to keep the dogs moving. And when there was soft snow into which the sledge runners sank and bogged, we plodded alongside urging the dogs forwards. But for the whole journey, smooth and rough, we were inside Christmas. Ulayuk's father sang in happiness, strange tuneless rhythms with words that I could never understand. As if he were beating a drum in his throat, or calling to the spirits with the pulse of his body. When I asked him what a song was, he said, "Kuviannarmat. It is because of the happiness."

On the second day of the journey I heard Eva, distant, her voice sounding from within the beating of the song of the man beside me on the sledge. When I heard her I leapt off and ran ahead of the dogs, to be closer to her, to make her fully audible. But her voice faded into the whiteness of the sea ice, into the distance.

Early on the fourth day the sledges all stopped alongside the steep cliffs of a headland. Everyone gathered together in excitement: the mission village would come into sight around the point. Sledge loads were reordered and lashed in perfect tidiness. Dogs' harnesses were untangled. And we all smoothed our fur suits, arranged our appearances.

Thus we arrived. The dogs raced across the last bay to the beach below the mission, drawn by the smells of other dogs, food and people. The church bell tolled. It was Christmas Eve.

Paulus was waiting for me. He caught my arm as I stepped up the shore, leading me away from Ulayuk, the unloading of the sledges, the hunters with their furs. "Welcome, welcome. Come. We have so much to talk about. I see they have dressed you as a savage!"

Back again in my room, in my place.

That night Paulus and I ate together. He told me that he had sent and received Christmas messages. All was well back home. My face burned. Arriving from so long in the air — not just the journey, but from the air that is life in the camps — and seated now in the mission, beside a fire, my face burned. With the heat. And with shame. There was nothing I could tell this man. I knew only that I must wait for the new year.

On Christmas Day, the mission servants pulled on their most European clothes and puffed at their brass instruments, and everyone sang. A week later the dog teams pulled their new loads, heavy with all that had been exchanged for furs at the mission store, out across the bay, round the point, and towards the camps.

Paulus had said, "You have learned enough. Now you might stay here, with us, for a while. The worst of the winter is to come. It would be easier for you here." It would have been impossible for me to stay! "No, no, I will spend a few weeks in the camps. My vocabulary is not yet good enough. Then, of course, I shall be here. Here, in the warm confines, where we will be able to talk so much more." He smiled at me, knowingly? I am not sure. But as I stood, again in my furs, beside

Ulayuk's family, at the shore, he said, "Be sure to return soon." And he stood there, watching us leave. He stood and he watched until he was no more than a thin mark against the snow. No one else was there. No life but his in the distance. For a moment I thought, that is how Christ should have appeared.

The worst of the winter did come. Not the cold: my clothes were a complete security against all outer bitterness. Ulayuk added polar bear hide to the souls of my caribou skin boots, so that I could stand beside seal holes and still not shuffle at the cold eating into my feet. Seals, it had been explained to me long since, see little but hear all. And when a broken seam in the hood of my caribou skin jacket let in the air — icy needles piercing the flesh! — Ulayuk ran a new seam of sinew thread over the old, and the suit was perfect again. Even on the coldest days a short walk would make me sweat, and I soon learned to imitate the hunters in their readiness to flap the tails of their jackets, throw back their hoods, take off gloves and even strip down to a single layer of caribou hide in order to avoid the real danger of overheating. Wetness, not cold, I learned, was the real enemy. And faces white with hoarfrost were warm faces: the body's heat caused moisture that became the startling whiteness on and around our heads: halos of inner comfort!

The cold was as much an ally as a foe. My real enemy was shame. The quarter light of a seal oil lamp; the long, long nights buried in a heap of skins at the edge of the sleeping platform; the torpor of waiting for storms to die down and the hunt to resume; the heavy satiety of great feasts of seal meat — these all left me alongside Ulayuk, feeling her open warmth always ready to receive me. Gentleness, companionship. And then the possibility for a time without shame: in her, everything could, for a time, be forgotten. Only to be remembered. Against this, I sought to pray. I looked for Eva in my prayers.

But, I thought, all would, in the end, be well: *Harmony* would arrive, Eva would be there. In her I could be my full self — not this half creature lost in an infinity of snow and ice. I stood outside and called to her. I wrote to her. Letters that I would present her when she stepped off the boat onto a summer shore. But I never turned to Ulayuk and said, tell your father that now it is time for me to return to the mission.

Winter was beginning to turn into early spring. "Early spring" — one of the six seasons of Ulayuk's people. Upingaksaak. The time of year distinctive for the wildness of its weather. We were stormbound in our snowhouses for day after day. We lay and slept and ate and played games. Jumping and pulling games. A version of blind man's buff. Spearing small bones. Even tickling. No one seemed concerned with winning any of these contests; there was pleasure in differences amongst us as well as in extremes of ability.

Once, as we all lay heaped against one another, panting after a series of tests of strength, Ulayuk's mother turned to me and asked, could Christians change the weather? No, I said. And thought, here is an occasion to explain the truth of Christianity, to inveigh against these people's heathen beliefs. For I knew that they believed that they, the people, could, if they must, if their lives depended on it, change the weather.

Ulayuk had once told me about Sila. "It is our word for weather," she said, "but she is a person." I said, "The spirit of the air?" She said, "Almost. But you white men, you Christians, do not know. You laugh at us." Then she told me that Sila, the spirit of the air, would at times move close to the camps, would sweep over the land. "When she comes," said Ulayuk, "storms come with her." And she told me that Sila came as a result of some wrongdoing, some breaking of the laws. Perhaps a woman had cooked caribou meat in a pot designed for cooking seal meat. Perhaps a hunter had failed to offer to the spirit of a newly killed seal a drink of fresh water. Ulayuk told me about these rules, and something of the consequence of indifference to them.

So could Christians change the weather? We know that there are no such things as weather spirits or seal souls. We know, instead, the power of God and Jesus. I should have said this out loud. But as I saw the eyes of the people searching my face for my real answer to Ulayuk's mother's question, I said nothing. Or merely repeated, no, we couldn't. And I waited.

"We can," said Ulayuk. "I know," I said. And then her mother asked, "Do you want to hear the drum?" The drum? Paulus had told me that the drum was, at last, no longer a part of people's life on this coast. A form of devil worship that, drum by drum, had been destroyed. The very last ones, he said, had come from the northern edge of the coast, and had been brought to him as trade items; they were now in the mission house, part of a collection of curios that Paulus had shown me when I first arrived there. No, I thought, I must not hear the drum. "Yes," I said, "I want to hear it." "Then come with us to Atagutaluk's house."

I went there and sat at the edge, beside the drying racks and lamp, and heard the drum and the songs and power of Atagutaluk the dreamer. Despite the line of burning mosses that were the stone lamp's wick, the snowhouse was dark. The figure of the drummer, at the centre of the sleeping platform, merged with a heap of skins and furs. Around him, between him and me, were silhouettes and glinting eyes. In this dark, a spirit was summoned, called into the body of the drummer. He shook with its realization. He called with its voice. He fell under its weight, the drum thumping to the floor. He struggled with it on the platform, hurling skins about him, calling with his voice, responding

to its high-pitched shrieks. I could understand none of the words —
if they were words — yet understood everything. Here was an
encounter between the soughing of the wind and the soul of the
hunter. A blasphemy for me even to witness; to remain silent . . . to
ignore this evil superstition . . . to be a part thereof . . . to risk a
contamination of belief . . .

After the spirit removed itself from Atagutaluk's body, he sat silent for
a long time, then gathered up his drum and sang as if to himself, as if
to recover his own being, as if none of us others were there. We visitors
returned to our own houses. Soon Ulayuk and I were on our sleeping
platform, under our sleeping robes. Sleep came. But in the night I
woke and reached out. I pulled Ulayuk towards me, feeling her skin
against mine, combatting the darkness, the strange terrors of the
drumming, of the spirit world. Ulayuk awoke. "Aukka, aukka," she
murmured. "It is against the rules, after the drum. We must wait two
nights." Still I clung to her, though she rolled around in my grasp, and
slept. Still I clung to her, pressing against the skin, pushing against the
darkness.

The next day the storms abated, the hunters set out. I went with them.
We followed frozen cracks, searching the endless expanses of sea ice
for mounds the size of snow buntings, where snow had gathered over
the openings of the seals' breathing holes. Soon we were all dots to one
another, each waiting for the sigh of the seal's breath, for the second
sound, the inhalation — the moment to plunge the harpoon down.
And soon there were shouts in the distance: seals were coming to be
taken, offering themselves to us. And as we hauled the bodies across
the snow, Atagutaluk went first, calling and laughing to the others.

Here, in the care of our nurses and orderlies, we eat two meals each day, at precise hours. Breakfast and lunch. For supper those who wish can help themselves to bread and jam. Those of us who rave are spoon fed in our cells, arms held in the thongs of the strait jackets.

At every meal there are prayers. We thank our God for his munificence. Each afternoon we receive the attentions of a servant of God, whole in mind, who asks us one by one if we have any matters that we feel we must discuss. Today I told him I could not believe in these arrangements. "Believe?" he said. "With faith there is no need to have *belief*, for we instead have knowledge." I made no reply.

When the cold of early spring yielded to the warmth of full spring, snowhouses were abandoned. Not without reluctance! For a while Ulayuk's father stretched his tent over the walls of snow blocks — the roof having fallen in or been taken down to save us from the constant dripping onto our heads and bedding. Then even the walls began to crumble, and the tent was taken off the remains of our snowhouse and pitched as a tent: a cone of sealskins arranged over driftwood branches. Sometimes a seal oil lamp was lit inside, but often we gathered twigs and wood to make fires at the entrance way.

In this new damp and warmth we changed our clothes. Caribou hide garments were packed away. We dressed in sealskin. Boots made from the bearded seal, for they are the most durable and waterproof, their seams all double stitched. Trousers and jackets from seal or sailcloth or oilskin. I missed the soft comfort of the caribou fur, the inner place that winter clothing had offered. Though it was some respite from the activities of the lice that found a perfect habitat living in the fur and feeding on our bodies.

Now we went fishing for codling and sculpin — strange spiked and ugly things; I learned with little wonder that the people called them Satan's creatures. We caught them through cracks and leads in the shore ice. Every day some of the men set out to look for seals, harpooning them as they surfaced in their exposed breathing holes or as they lay basking out on the ice. Along the headlands we found colonies of gulls, and helped ourselves to their brown and black splashed eggs. Ducks and geese arrived. And the tundra burst into colour. Every day was a feast of air and light and meat.

Twice we moved our tent, hauling everyone and everything. First to the mouth of a river to spear arctic char. They swarmed in their thousands, their movements boiling the water's surface. These were the fish, Ulayuk said, on their way from lakes far inland to summer feeding grounds at sea. And then we moved to a spit of land where the ice was good, and gave access to the dozing seals. When we travelled, I saw that the dogs left smears of blood at every pace, their paws cut on ice thawed into blades and spikes by the heat of the sun. I said to Ulayuk, "The dogs are bleeding. Will they not be lame?" She said, "Wait and see." That night the men fashioned tiny boots — scarcely more than flaps of sealskin — and the next morning tied them onto those dogs whose paws left the largest stains of blood in their tracks.

After the second move, Atagutaluk spoke of the distant spring hunting grounds, the place where uncertainty of broken ice was avoided, the place where many times people's lives had been safest, the place where, in summer, caribou could be found. A better place. But far away. "We should go there," he said. Ulayuk asked me if I was ready for this long move. I said, "We should not be so far from the mission." Ulayuk said,

"You are right. It is safer to be near a trading store." She was silent for a moment. Then she said: "If you return to the mission, and we are not too far away, I can visit you." "Yes," I said. "Yes."

I understand, now, here in the hospital, having had time — so much time — to consider the drums and chanting and magic of Atagutaluk. The dream, or the vision, is the divide between two places. The other, far place, is beyond our reach. But from the dream, from the divide, from the height of the inner land, we can see some distance over there. The journey to this vantage point is both difficult and essential. Few can undertake it with sufficient skill, can gain high enough ground, to be able to see the vital places. What are these places? Where animals come from, where their spirits reside. The reasons for failure; where its essences can be found. The outlines of the future; where what must happen can be glimpsed.

Yesterday I told the cook about Atagutaluk. I said, I had the dream and am now inside it. I told him about the drum, about the pulse of dreams. I explained that it was possible to live in another kind of landscape. He did not appear to be much interested.

But that night I dreamed of the divide. Paulus and I were travelling along the ice. The ice was the divide. My etchings were, for me, what visions of animals and failure and the future are for Atagutaluk. A permanent vision.

At the sealing camp out on the spit, Paulus came to visit me — to look for me, rather. Travelling in the endless day of the Inuit spring, he arrived on a sledge driven by Kusugak, the mission servant. We saw them arrive in the far and glimmering distance, against the blues and greens of meltwater that now spread over the cracking sea.

As they came up to the camp, I noticed the vividness of Paulus's face, in part red and inflamed, in part bronzed, by the wind and sun. As he looked at me, I realized how much darker I would be than him, how much wilder than he could have expected, and how little I had thought of such things since we last had seen one another, at the mission, at Christmas. I knew that he had come to take me back there with him. And, even before his long strides had brought him beside our tents, I knew that I must acquiesce. He did not need to explain that before long the ice would be rotten or gone, and that it would no longer be possible to make the journey by dog team. He did not need to warn me of the risk of being caught out at camps for the length of the summer, for the journey by kayak would be far too hazardous for a European to attempt. He did not have to detail the likely schedules for the *Harmony*, or tell me that of course I must be there, at the dock, when she first arrived, to welcome my wife to be.

No, I caught Paulus's hand and said how good it was to see him at last, and that I had been wondering how I was to make my long overdue return to the mission. But I could not conceal my vigour, my pride. I had to show him our camp, explain our hunting, take him visiting each family. As if he had seen none of it before, in his thirty years as a missionary on that coast! He indulged me by staying two nights with us before setting off.

The return was long and slow. We were obliged to make long detours around leads in the ice too wide for Kusugak's sledge. Often we travelled through a shallow expanse of meltwater. And the dogs' feet were cut and cut by the melting ice. We limped along, moving when we could in the coldest part of the day or night, taking advantage of whatever new ice gave a fast surface for our journey. For much of the time we walked alongside or behind the dogs. Only in the deepest water did we sit, side by side, on the loaded sledge.

Paulus tried to talk to me. He tried to warn me. He explained, over and over, the nature of the missionary venture. He urged me with questions to be clear about what I must accept.

He said: "Is this a task, a land, for which you are suitably prepared?"

"Now," I said; "now I am indeed prepared. Now I am ready to give my life to these people, this task. Now I know what the coming years will require of me."

My enthusiasm was boundless. Paulus listened to me. Listened and watched. Saying, from time to time, "Are you sure, then? Are you sure you are ready for the sacrifices? The acceptance of the common good? The loss of self?"

"Yes, yes!" I was sure. Yet I knew nothing of what he knew was in store for me. "Yes, I am sure I can make my life here. Nowhere else, nowhere else!" I wonder, as he watched me, if he was infected with my conviction. I believe so. For at times he patted me on the arm or shoulder, as if to endorse my enthusiasm, as if to share in my energy, and said quietly, "I do believe you will manage." I never thought to wonder what he thought I would have to *manage*.

I play chequers against my fellow men. We sit in our rooms, one against one, seeking to turn our pieces into kings or queens. Trying to jump a way to the other end, and then double back for the kill. A game of crude metaphors. My favourite opponent is the cook — he has a rare energy for the game, and his white costume belongs to menial work, not to the domain of strait jackets and sedation. Other inmates here are, for the most part, too disturbed to achieve, still less maintain, the tactical skill to make the game the necessary struggle. And when I become too disturbed, and my tactics are nonsensical, the cook merely takes quick advantage, demolishing my little men in a few minutes, laughing with triumph, and then, to console me, tells me with surprising enthusiasm the culinary delights to be offered in today's lunch.

Yesterday — a bad day — my game against the cook ended with him declaring: "Peas, my dear Heinrich, fresh garden peas. To go with Bavarian ham. Your favourite!"

Paulus and I played chequers every night as we waited for the *Harmony* to appear. That year the ice was slow to break and disperse: entry to the bay was impossible for anything but the people's kayaks. We sat at his study window, making our moves, and casting glances at the white horizon.

— "Your life, Heinrich, is in God's hands."

I looked out at the black and jagged lines of the sea, opening its way to our ship.

— "There is much that will be hard for you."

I watched the gulls that hovered and dropped to the water's edge.

— "Tomorrow is midsummer's day. Soon she will be here."

She? The *Harmony*? Or Eva?

— "Your wife to be."

Dusk came at midnight, dawn before three. No amount of ice could hold out against the ever circling heat of the midsummer sun.

In the daytime I worked on a house for us. Post and beam. Rough planks and panels. Two rooms. One with a great tin stove. The other with a wide bed. Paulus helped me in this work; his carpentry was as precise and elegant as his turns of phrase. Kusugak and the other servants of the mission hauled materials, pounded nails and pegs, cut joints and assembled a strong roof. Paulus offered, on behalf of his wife, by raiding her cupboards, fabrics for curtains and gave me — should I say us? — a rocking chair.

As we at last assembled the headboard of the wide bed, Paulus remarked: "She will bring linen and, I believe, a new mattress."

I said, "You have been in touch with her!"

"Yes, indeed, indirectly. We get messages back and forth."

"But I could have sent word!"

"You were out in the camps. Learning your Eskimo language."

There was a pause. Paulus said: "You can not imagine how many times I attempted to get some message to you!"

On the day the new cabin was declared to be finished — which meant, simply, that Paulus and Kusugak and the others left the work to me alone — the ice in the bay vanished. I woke, looked out as always at what I expected to be the usual maze of colour and ice pans, and was astounded to find nothing before me but the sea. I rushed out of the mission, down to the shore, and stared at the rippling blueness of it, hearing in my ears the wild cries of gulls and terns as they threw themselves at the surface of this unexpected water. Lumps of greyish sand-pitted ice littered the tide edge. But these, and the winter they recalled, were irrelevant beside the open water. Open water. Another summer. The time for boats, supplies, change.

That night Ulayuk and her family appeared. They had travelled in by skin boats. I saw them at the shoreline unloading a tent and piling their goods beyond the water's reach. I turned back into my cabin, continued my carving and hammering. Then Ulayuk was at the door. From the floor, amid the wood chips and sawdust, I looked up at her. She smiled. She said, "See, we were camped not too far away. Even Atagutaluk is with us."

I said, "My wife will be arriving."

She said, "Yes." And, looking round the inside of the cabin: "She will be happy to have this good house."

I said, "Ulayuk."

She said, "I hope she will like me. I will visit her when we are here."

I said, "It is not allowed. Only the missionaries can come into these houses."

She said, "Then you must bring her to visit me. My father says he wants to meet her. He thinks she will be like you."

She paused. "My father says he misses you."

But as I worked on the cabin, I heard Eva approaching, coming closer. At last I longed for her. At last our vows could be honoured. We would kiss one another. Suddenly, after all this waiting, I could wait no longer. Two nights after the sea had opened, I dreamed of her.

Eva lay on my new bed, but there was no mattress. The rough boards cut into her. She rolled on them, groaning. She ran her bare arms along the wood. I stood beside the bed, dressed in my winter furs, my head covered by the hood of the parka, watching her, desiring her. I thought: now is the consummation. She reached up to me. She called to me. She opened her mouth, summoning me to enter. I leant over her, to kiss her. Her arms reached up and her hands caught hold of the skin — she seized the caribou hair and pulled me furclad onto her. Tighter and tighter she held me, forcing the breath from my lungs. She pressed her face to mine, her mouth to mine, saying, "It is agreed, then. At last it is agreed."

I woke, panting and gasping for air. And I longed for my Eva. That day I walked far along the edge of the new sea, then climbed high onto the headland, and looked out beyond the closed bay, to the islet mottled horizon, to the channels through which the ship would come. And on the wind I heard her voice, a song to me, calling. A lament. Released from the ice, belonging, as I thought, to this land, given its permission to love freely, I yearned for her. How I yearned for her!

A week later, hardly before I was accustomed to the change of season, I woke in the new cabin at dawn and looked out to find the *Harmony* at anchor in the bay. She seemed so huge. Dinghies and whale boats and kayaks were hastening to get alongside her. And at the *Harmony*'s rail I could make out a line of figures. I searched their shapes with my eyes. I thought I saw the billow of a dress. Yes, it must be Eva. Antlike figures were moving in the rigging, and the ship's boat was lowered alongside, making ready, I supposed, for the first visit to our little community. As I watched, the mission bell tolled, and our people began running to the shore. I joined them. Everyone was shouting. I shouted, too. I called, in madness, "Eva! Eva!"

As I stood at the landing point, Kusugak came to me. He touched my elbow. He said, "She is here already." Yes, I replied, here at last. "With Dr Paulus. In his study." What? Where? "They arrived in the night. They came ashore first. The women. Dr Paulus's wife. And yours."

I turned and ran back up the beach, past my cabin, on to the mission building where Paulus had his study. Through its heavy doorway, up the wooden stairs . . . At Paulus's study door I froze. My heart beat, I was unable to think, to speak. I was aware of the murmur of voices from the other side of the door. I tried to breathe. I closed my eyes and prayed. I touched my face, my hair. I wiped the sweat from me. I touched my eyes open with my fingers, breathed again, and knocked. The murmur of voices ceased. There was a silence. I waited. Silence then slow footsteps. Paulus opened the door. He filled the doorway, obscuring the interior. "Ah, Heinrich. Kusugak found you. I had hoped to talk with you . . ." But I said, "Eva. She's here." And moved towards him, towards the body that blocked my way. "Heinrich . . . You'd better come in."

Two women stood there, at the table by the window, looking at me from the far side of the room. I noticed their hands on the table, each on one side, as if to steady themselves. One was elderly, thin and grey and in the grip of some unspeakable anxiety: her twisted face stared at me. The other was much younger, fair haired, strong looking. She offered me a pale smile.

— "Eva?"

She was not there.

Paulus followed me into the room. He took my arm. He introduced me. "My wife, Elizabeth." She took my hand and squeezed it. "And Martha, your betrothed." Martha reached out her hand, held mine for a moment, then raised hers to her chest. "This is our dear Heinrich."

— "Eva?"

I stared about me, I looked back at the door, at the window. She was not there.

I screamed the question at him: "Where is she? WHERE IS SHE?" Paulus turned to the two women. "Perhaps you would excuse us for a while." And they moved to the door, opened it, and slid away — though Martha turned, as she left, and said, "I hope that I will have some time, also, to explain things to you, Heinrich. I would like that." She was so strong from the very beginning. And clear.

In my game of chequers with the cook I hurl the pieces to the ground.
I beat my fists on the table. I leap to my feet. My chair crashes to the
ground behind me. He says: "Pigs' trotters in a perfect broth. With
parsley." I lift my fists to pound his face. "And new rye bread." I smash
down again on the table, on the chequerboard. The door to my dark
room opens. Two men come in and seize me, wrestle me to the ground,
forcing my arms into the sleeves of the white jacket. I fight them,
panting, wretched, wordless.

"You must listen to me most carefully, Heinrich. I am speaking to you
of your profoundest obligations."

I listened. And listened. He said, over and over, in many ways, the
simple things:

"All that takes place now rests with you. It is our wish, it is my wish,
that you marry Martha. Take your time. Be confident that we have not
chosen with caprice, without your particular needs in mind. Do not
judge her but for her actual qualities. Do not carry your disappointment into your dealings with her. Occupy yourself with your work
here. Your house. Your duties. Make use of your new skills as a speaker
of the people's language; consolidate your experience of, your intimacy
with, the way of life out there on the land and the ice. Work as a
missionary. As an interpreter for God. No one will be better placed
than you for this task. Take your time. Devote your attentions to our
trading. You understand the hunter; now become the trader. One side
of your self in place here; ensure that the other side, your complement,

finds *its* place. Take your time. And, eventually, as a full and strong member of our community, you will be able to share a full and strong life with your wife, with Martha. She, I can assure, will expect you to take your time." You had such faith in time.

He also said:

"You need not forget Eva. That which is hidden from memory lurks there, and prepares to take its revenge!" You laughed at this conception of the mind. "Understand her as your first love, the enthusiasm of the youth who, with all his wildness, knows too little of the limits, the constraints of adult manhood. Understand her as the beauty, the singer — for all that she was for you. And understand her, also, for that which she was not: reliable, practical, the complement to the missionary. Martha can be what few ever could: a good wife. In choosing your vocation here, you chose a life where each of us must have a fullness of being, a stature before our fellow men and — of course — before God. Yes, stature."

He also said:

"With Eva you could never have stood tall and proud and complete. This we know better than you. And we know what flows from incompleteness: it is to place at risk our entire endeavour."

I listened, and did as I was asked.

Martha visited me in the new house. We worked together, nailing boards for the floor, assembling shutters for the windows, arranging stones and planks to make a walkway between the house and the other buildings of the mission. We sat side by side at church services. I interpreted for her when she wished to have dealings with the local women. We took walks together on Sunday afternoons, during which she picked the leaves and flowers of the tiny alpine plants that she discovered on bare hillsides and along the shores: she made a collection, pressed and labelled with their scientific and Inuttut names. And she exclaimed with delight at the sight of a sea bird with its young, or a glimpse of a whale rolling and spouting out in the bay. But we said nothing of our plight. The betrothal received no acknowledgement. She appeared to expect nothing. She must have hoped for everything.

She talked about herself only once. She said little. She said she came from Scotland, that she had been a domestic, a person who lived by caring for children in rich homes. She said she believed in God and destiny. And that she had always known she would live, one day, as a missionary's wife. Where had she met Paulus? Where had he found her? She shrugged. She said she had joined the Moravians. So of course they had met. She said she was orphaned, had always been orphaned. She said I should understand that she knew enough to believe she could love me well. But for the most part, most often, she was silent.

The first snows of a new autumn began to tighten our lives. Our walks became circumscribed. The house, finished, provided a place to which we could retreat and warm ourselves. In the confines of impending winter — and in anticipation, no doubt, of ever greater confinement in the months ahead — we experienced one another's solitudes. With a yearning to relieve loneliness by a sharing of it, we married.

The wedding, despite music played by two lines of mission Inuit for whom the brass band represented the deepest expression of Christian zeal, was a sombre event. Paulus led us out of the church. We stood for a moment, looking out at the bay. The year's new ice had finally

E v a

quieted the sea. I thought, soon it will be possible to travel again to the people's winter camps.

After the wedding, the marriage. Paulus said, "Heinrich, you have the perfect wife."

Martha had broad shoulders, large hands. She wore dark, heavy clothes; her hair tied in a bundle under a wool scarf. Yet her strength was supple, her hair luxuriant. Beneath her deftness in everyday work and her commitment to duty, she was gentle. By the most caring and careful nudges she tried to steer me towards her.

She expected nothing, but made me welcome — welcome to keep her at my side, to take her into my arms. I did feel the warmth of her offers and knew, also, my duty. In the first days of our marriage we became husband and wife. She hugged me to her, laid her cheek on mine, saying, "You are so dear to me. Dearest. Dearest."

She made me remember Eva. And I hated Martha's goodness. I could never learn to love her. She knew it. She often said, "We have a life to make together." At night, when we lay together, I would close my eyes. So tight that my face crumpled. As does a small child's when surprised by a bitter taste. Then, in fierce blindness, I would remove myself to the screen, be among the etchings, among the ghosts. With Ulayuk. Then my penis swelled, and I felt her embrace. My hips moved. Further, fuller, I would join with the images behind my eyes. And then, from among the whiteness, from the distance, without connection, ghost possessed, I could spurt my semen into Martha. And I awoke, returning to the actual separation, hopelessness in every pore of my skin.

69

Here, in the dark rooms, in prayer and confession, even in the endless games of chequers with the cook, I am inert. In the pit of my being lie stones. Like a creature in a sack, weighted in readiness to be drowned. They tell me, "This is your illness." I say to them, "It is no more than the places where we reside."

As the year of my married life came into winter, Martha and I lived in our new house. I fetched armfuls of pine trees and hacked them into logs for our stove. I went to the church and preached in the language of the north to those families who remained too attached to our mission to be able to resume or continue their lives in the winter sealing camps. Between making firewood and sermons there was nothing. I hung limp in a chair. I stared out into the bay. I sank — sack full of stones that I became — deeper and deeper into some limpid body of still water. Water that muffled all sounds and excluded all interference.

Paulus visited us. "Ah," he said. "You are finding the opportunity to consider life. A good thing. Use the opportunity well." I used it. Martha knew, from the beginning, that she was faced by inertia, not thought. With her usual gentleness she invited me to talk, to walk, to help make small improvements. Then to read, even. To prepare my Inuttut preaching.

Paulus visited us more. He began to worry about me. "Heinrich," he said. "You have spent long enough taking stock. It is time to begin trading." I looked at him, wondering but not asking if he had in mind trade at the mission store or some more symbolic meaning.

Then the voices began again. Eva singing outside our house, in the dark of midwinter. It must have been Christmas time: I remember that Ulayuk had come with her family for their visit to the church and store. I watched them from the window of the new house. And the next day I watched them again, as they made ready to set off on two sledges, loaded with flour and sugar and tea and tobacco and rifle ammunition. They were returning to the land.

I too hoped to return to the land. Martha and Paulus told me to go. My stillness was unbearable to them both. For their different reasons. Paulus came to visit, in April. The days were already long. Hunters would soon be travelling by night, when the surface of their world was hard and the beating of the sun less relentless. Paulus and I talked about the camps, the way in which the people remained there, beyond the reach of our mission. He said he suspected that they practised their heathenism. He wondered if I might be ready to make another journey to the camp of Ulayuk and her family. Might I not persuade Atagu-taluk, that old curmudgeon (I remember Paulus used this very English term, part abuse, part affection, utterly superior), to lead his small community in Christian prayer. "Make a catechist of him," said Paulus. "Give him a sense of importance in our scheme of things. Then he'll come round, won't he?" He told me that it was a task for which I was perfectly suited, having sat for so long pondering this and connected matters. He made jokes to conceal his extreme apprehension.

And Martha. She was lonely, but must by then have been thinking her solitude would be lessened by my absence. Silence is the least companion. And it reproached her, always, for not being Eva. I suppose she continued to believe that Eva was the cause of my inertia. And when I heard the singing, and held my hands over my ears, and screamed out for silence, I never told Martha that I hated these sounds as much as she must have done. I wanted Eva to go away, to stay away. She got in the way of my dreams.

So Martha said to me, "Do as Father Paulus suggests." (She always referred to him as father; encouraging obedience in us.) "Stay out in the camps as long as you need. I shall manage here." She was pregnant.

I threw myself at the door of those in charge. I shouted at them, "I have done nothing criminal, nothing that anyone has found me guilty of. I must leave here." They opened the door. They gave me a hearing. We talked politely, at length, about the appropriateness of confession. This huge confessional! I said, "Very well, I confess." "To what?" they asked. "To having lost my way. To failing in our mission." I urged them to let me go, to let me return to the town of my childhood. I said, "I must see Eva, my original fiancée. Do you care nothing for her feelings?" "She is well enough," they said. I urged them to believe that I had a life out there, beyond these walls, where there is not darkness, where there are horizons, albeit the close forms of our ordinary world. They said, "You do not have the freedom to decide." I shouted at them, "But you do!" "No," they said. "It is not in our power." "Then I am a prisoner!" "Yes," they said. "Yes, you are." And as an afterthought, following a long silence: "But then, aren't we all? Prisoners of some form of duty, that is."

In the last week of April, Atagutaluk came in to the mission with one of the children of their camp, a little girl who had pierced her hand with a harpoon. The wound was infected. The child's hand was purple and swollen. Paulus called me as interpreter and comforter. He was sure the treatment of the wound would cause shrieks of protest or pain or both. Nor did he trust Atagutaluk — rather, he feared him: our efforts to heal, said Paulus, would be an inevitable if implicit reproach against those practised by Atagutaluk. So we all gathered in the mission anteroom.

Atagutaluk handed the child to me, and I handed her to Paulus. Atagutaluk moved to the very back of the room, and squatted against the wall. Paulus produced a lance, white spirit of alcohol, and a great roll of bandage. The child stared into his eyes, saying nothing. Paulus gave directions, offered descriptions and explanations, waiting between each sentence for me to translate. He was eager to impress the subdued Atagutaluk. I translated.

The pressure of words was so great as to leave no moment for the child to speak. Yet she gave no inclination to do so. She accepted the pain — it must have been terrible! Even as the lance cut into her swollen hand she no more than blinked, though Paulus said, "Tell her it will hurt now, but she must be brave. Be brave little one, be brave." And when he dabbed on the searing antiseptic, she closed her eyes, and her little body shuddered, but she let out no sound. "Be good, little girl. The pain is for your good. God is watching over us. We are doing his work. Be sure to tell her this, Heinrich, tell her God is helping us here." And no sound, no form of complaint, from either the girl or the dreamer.

The next day Atagutaluk sent me a message. He was returning to the camp. Did I want to go with him? Paulus had already seen the opportunity. He himself helped take supplies to Atagutaluk's sledge. And Martha . . .

Martha urged me to go, to carry on the work. She would be well, she said, and happy to anticipate my return before the ice left the bays. She smiled. Strong in her sense of obligation. Fatalistic, perhaps. Or at peace in her pregnancy, in readiness for her very own Christmas.

I went again today to my superiors, or doctors, or gaolers. I told them I was not a criminal. I am responsible for evil. I can atone outside this confinement. I told the cook, "I can bear it no longer. I have served my time." I refused to play chequers against him. He told me there was a vegetable broth for lunch.

Atagutaluk's sledge creaked and bumped over the spring ice. Melt-water had not yet formed. The world was white, with a brilliance beyond compare. We travelled timelessly, stopping to eat, to sleep, to rest as mood dictated. I was back in the etched images, in the domain between me and the far horizons, climbing again to a vantage point from which to see. And at last I did see. Not in the drum, or in sleep, but alongside Atagutaluk, on the sledge. We talked of what I saw.

Jesus had come. After all this waiting, his promise was fulfilled. The angels summoned me, urged me to be ready. To make everyone ready. Jesus and God were close, very close. Atagutaluk was Jesus.

I told him who he was. I passed on the messages of the angels. He smiled at me, nodding, agreeing. Beside us, as if in confirmation of a miracle, the little girl slept, her bandaged hand no longer purple with gangrene. We prepared ourselves for the camp. I told Atagutaluk of his power, and of our mission. Jesus was here. God would come to us. From the sun. Over the ice. Striding, bursting through the whiteness. We would all have joy.

I said, "We will be naked before God." Atagutaluk looked at me, then up at the sun. "Jesus, God's son, will he be naked?" "Yes," I said. "Yes, he the first, before all others." Then Atagutaluk gave a great guffaw, set his long whip into the lashing of the sledge, and pulled off his atigi, the caribou hide jacket that drew over his head and beneath which his upper body was naked. He looked up again at the sun, and called out: "We are warm down here!" He laughed. But I felt the strength of his understanding as sure as the strength of his hunter's body.

For the last two days of our journey, we struggled over ice that was layered with a foot of new snow. The seals' breathing holes were buried. The sledge would not travel, its runners sinking too deep for the dogs to be able to pull. Exhausted, we arrived at the camp.

The new snow was everywhere, blown back and forth by spring storms. Travel with dogs was impossible. Even the strongest men staggered and forced themselves against the storm, had to endure the weight of soft and unseen drifts against each step they took. In the blizzards the hunters struggled to keep a sense of direction. We were blinded by whiteness. Some searched for fish in lakes inland. Others dug out old caches along the beaches. But the food was not there.

When the storm abated, the new-blown snow concealed the world, dogged our steps. Day after day the hunting failed. The women sat very quiet beside their lamps, whose flames guttered and expired as the oil sank to a smear. Small children stayed close to their mothers for warmth, for protection that could not, in the end, be given to them. The men came in at the end of fruitless hours, hollow cheeked, their eyes bright with apprehension. Hunger clawed at our entrails. At night we lay long and dreamed of banquets. We were starving.

Ulayuk said to me, "Now you understand how we have lived, with uncertainty." I said, "Perhaps you should have gone to spring camp, to the place far away, to where the caribou can be found." She said, "We need to be near you. We need the mission."

Atagutaluk visited the houses, explaining that the angels had passed along a message, that I understood that he, Atagutaluk, was Jesus. That this was salvation, the end of hunger, what the white man could bring. And one night he took out his drum and pounded and sang his spirit way to the new discovery of his power. I remember, with terrible intensity, the drum. The man's voice. Ulayuk's presence beside me. The glimmer of light in the cracks of the snowhouse. The glow of the oil lamp. Each one of us there knew the truth, and testified. The little girl's hand, in its bandage, was our starting point. From there we made our way to visions. To find the origin of the animals, the reasons for hunger, the shape of the future.

Every night we drummed and sang. One morning, lying beside Ulayuk on the sleeping platform, I told her of Atagutaluk's new power. About Jesus in him. About salvation. "I know," she murmured to me.

"I know. But we, the Inuit, are dying here." "I can help you. There is hope with your Jesus." "Jesus is yours, not ours," she said. "But now he is yours. More yours than anyone's. Through Atagutaluk, in the drum." "If this will save us," she said, "tell us how." "When?" "With Atagutaluk, after the drum."

All the supplies I had brought, that Paulus had helped me load on the sledge, were finished. Our hunger was terrible.

For the first time I spoke as a missionary to these people, to Ulayuk's people. I said, in their language, with all the authority I could find, "Tomorrow we must be ready. We must go to meet God in the sun. In the sun on the ice." "Yes," said Atagutaluk. " We must go naked. And then there will be seals."

When Jesus is joined by God, then seals will be ready to give themselves up to the hunters.

Was this a crime? Was it not hope? A seeking for a remedy. A route to food. Life itself. I did not commit murder.

The next morning the day was clear. The winds had dropped. Soft snow lay on the ground. At dawn, the sun rose on the eastern rim of the sea ice. "This, now, is God's approach!" "Yes," they cried. "We must be naked." "Where will he come from?" "There, in the sun!" I said: "Naked in spirit, in soul." Atagutaluk said: "We must be naked." They called out: "We must be naked before God's approach!"

Many took off their clothes and ran into the rising light. I said to them, "Wait. Wait." Some turned and staggered back to the camp, shaking, convulsing. Some fell to their knees, then pitched forwards into the snow. They were taken. Ulayuk was the last to die, calling out to God as she froze. Calling into the sun.

Atagutaluk brought me with him, back to the snowhouse, onto the sleeping platform. I must have fainted, or slept. I woke to see Paulus looking down at me. He was shaking me. "Heinrich! Heinrich! Wake up." I thought, how have I returned to the mission? Is God with us now? "Heinrich! What is happening here?"

Paulus had come. Martha was losing her baby. I had to return to the mission. Kusugak was here with a dog team. They had plenty of supplies. They could leave food for people. We should return — he said it over and over, as I might not grasp his meaning — to the mission. Paulus told me that I must explain everything to him later. He had already heard, from Kusugak, of the deaths. We were not responsible, of course. Missionary work sometimes faltered. He said: "These people have a long way to go." He said: "Their understanding is so limited." He said, as an explanation: "A drum has been kept here, in defiance of the Church." He exonerated me: "You have tried your best, against great odds, to overcome superstition." He told me that I could see now the work that remained to be done. This was an unhappy episode. He insisted that there was no need to relate too much, certainly not the unsatisfactory details. Tragedy and failure provide lessons, but can also become, once digested, a closed book. Of course the police would want to interfere — were they to hear. They were not to hear. Did I understand? Yes, I understood. Kusugak could be trusted, of course, not to chatter about these events. He said: "This is our lesson, not everyone's story . . ."

On and on you went, Dr Paulus, with your fear. You knew what this could mean for the mission, or for me. We could all be disgraced. Ruined. Driven off the coast by rival traders, rival Christians. I could be accused of murder. Of all manner of crime. It would be so easy to misunderstand.

On and on you went, Dr Paulus. On the sledge as we lumbered back to Martha. In your book-lined room in the mission. And of course I must return to Germany. You would arrange a place for me to rest, an institution belonging to our Church, where remarkable cures were achieved. A place where I would be safe. Martha would remain on the coast. She was devoted to the Church, and would remain faithful to it and to me. In due time . . . In due time.

Martha cared for me during the time we waited for *Harmony* to appear again. The ice went out early. I began the journey south in the first week of July. As a traveller again. Through the sheltered in-shore passages down the coast, out over the Newfoundland Banks, across the huge Atlantic, down the Nordsee, through the Helgolander Bucht, up the estuary of the Elbe, to the flat docks of Hamburg. They took me to a horizonless room. This horizonless room.

"What use is my life? What can its purpose be? I chose to serve God. My vocation."

They replied to me: "You can serve God in prayer."

"I have no prayers, only memories. Where is my mission?"

I argued with them. I have argued with them for many years. And at last they have set me free.

Today I said goodbye to the cook. To the darkness. I walked out, through the slatted door, hardly more than a hatch set into the oak entrance way. Out, through the courtyard, through the gates onto the road. Out, into the city.

The rain fell in a cold drizzle. Over and over I said to myself, I have no guilt. I saw a motor car. I had never seen one before. Water splashed up from its wheels. The driver sounded a horn. I walked on. A cab, drawn by a thin, grey horse creaked by. I ran after the cab, shouting, "Ich müss mitfahren! I must drive with you!" I caught up and climbed in. The driver, high up and cloaked against the rain. "Wohin, wohin? Where to?"

A prayer should not end with a question. God needs his reassurances. I told the driver, "Mit ihnen und ihren. With you and yours." I shall make a journey as before, strong in my vocation, bringing to us here the etchings, the shadows on the screen.

From my vantage point on this cab, alongside the simple tasks of the driver, I can view the city. He will take me to the church. We will pray together. We shall hear the voices of the angels.

ISLAND

A green VW beetle is twisting its way along a thin road between cliff and beach. Marianne is driving, pulling the wheel back and forth, cutting the corners, dodging rocks in the road, bouncing through potholes. She says to herself: "I'm fleeing, fleeing for my life." On the seat beside her is a hold-all and a coat. Window wide open, she inhales the sea air deep into herself. Her blonde hair flaps around her face, which is wide and strong. She sings, her voice rough edged, untuneful.

> Mama, I'm going to have it out with you.
> Mama, I'm going to see it through with you.
> Mama, love me do.
> Mama . . . a . . . a . . . a love you through and through.

Marianne's energy rolls through the song. She forces the sound, as loud as she can, up from her lungs through her throat, guttural and shrieked, the effort making her cheeks stretch, her eyes narrow and blurred.

Mama, I'm going to have it out with you.
Just imagine, imagine what we could do.

She drives round a steep headland. The road, its edges littered with rockfall, is no wider than her car. Above her the cliff climbs up to the sky; below her it dives down, ragged and sheer, to the sea.

Imagine an island for the two of you.

She rounds a series of blind corners, one hand swirling the steering wheel. Her song is a roar from far inside her.

Stare at the sea, baby, stare at the sea.
Leaving my world behind.

Lost in the song, speeding with its sounds and rhythm, she meets a flock of sheep. Brakes scream. Dogs bark. Ewes bleat. A man yells. The car slams into the cliff and rebounds into the animals. A body jams under the front bumper — a soft, woolly brake. Marianne, crumpled inside the car, rolls her eyes and shouts:
   "Holy fuck!"

In my mind's eye, Ysobel stared out to sea. Ysobel. My mother. With her wide face and long hair. How old was she? How strange it was not to be able to be sure of her, of anything about her. Somewhere between middle aged and old, worn by life — by drunkenness. But her face was sensuous and her body was strong. A blend of hard and soft; I thought — I seem to have thought this since the beginning of time — either her age or her youth has never been resolved. I could not think of her as a mother; she came to mind, and suspended herself there, as Ysobel.
   The window frame around Ysobel was dappled with mould. Chintz curtains floated from a wooden rail.

Beyond the window, the sea was flat calm. Greased. Broken by island humps and peaks that fractured the smoothness of it all. Ysobel gazed at the greased sea, the islands, and beyond them to the long horizon.

In her, in her room, was dust in the light, the smell of seaweed, the slight sourness of empty bottles. She turned from the window and reached to a cupboard in the wall. With a long, silver-ringed finger she pushed the edge of the cupboard door. It swung open. She took a bottle, a glass, filled it with brown sherry. She drank and, glass empty, toasted the sea. A silent toast to the horizon.

She walked across the room, to a huge cabinet gramophone, a stack of records. She put on Connie Francis, scratchy, loud. Her mind filled with sad words and a bright tune. I loved Connie Francis, though she belonged to some other generation. "Stupid Cupid, stop picking on me."

Ysobel looked again at the sea, the islands, the distance.

She whispered to herself: "Marianne." A sound so quiet and yet so full of breath; muted but urgent. "Marianne. Marianne."

At the edge of the sea, waves sucked at flotillas of weed. Crabs scurried in the shallows of an incoming tide. A line of surf hissed back and forth. At the tideline, in the lie of a narrow beach, old buoys and fixings and ropes slopped about in the sea's drift.

Beside a keel-made scar in the sand stood a tall, strong young man. His skin seemed to be smoothed and warmed by sea air, reflected sun. Uistean! I knew him, for sure. He was standing beside a wooden boat fitted with an eight-horsepower outboard motor. His fishing boat. I wanted to call out to him, to let him know that I saw him there, so strong, so smooth. Words would not come.

He saw that the tide had moved another few yards. He grabbed up an anchor hanging from the boat's side, seized the bow and hauled the cumbersome thing up with the water. He tugged its weight beyond the surf, as far up the sand as he was able. He flung the anchor ahead of him, up onto the beach. The water slapped at the stern; the tide nudged on up. In a few minutes it would be time again to pull the boat towards the land.

Uistean wandered a few yards along the shore, sat on a rock, picked up a stone and flung it at a passing gull.

The large white house stood up like a photo-montage, a dream, a mistake: where a croft should be, a manor was stuck onto an island shore. Sheep wandered up to the front door. Most windows, elegant and Georgian, were shuttered or curtained. A blind edifice against the sky. Perched on a hillside of tight, short grass. Beyond, all around, was the sea.

From an upper window came the scratchy and incongruous sounds of Connie Francis. Ysobel stood there, staring out. She leaned forward, and screamed:

"George, George!! Marianne, I can see Marianne!"

On the shore, among marram grasses and outcrops of white rocks, a craggy, thin man in his sixties, crouched on hands and knees. A figure from the depths of the sea, of the past. Of course: George! So hard to recognize him in the grass. And over his grey hair he wore headphones. Around his shoulders was strapped a tape recorder. One hand clutched a muffled directional microphone. He was immobile, transfixed. Then he eased the microphone forwards, into the grasses. A second lead from his tape recorder disappeared into a nesting hole in a sandy bank. He listened and smiled most happily.

George's eyes were closing. Through the headphones, louder than any real life could offer, he heard the clucks and cheeps of a nestful of shelducks.

On the tape recorder, the little cassette turned in its silence, gathering up for this man an impression of chicks and ducks and sounds of wind in the grass.

A tractor and trailer grumbled along a lane, then turned through a farm gate onto a track leading to the shore. The tractor was driven by Conniach — ruddy-faced, long-nosed. I sat in the trailer. I clung to the rickety slats that made a rough side around me, and bounced up and down, up and down as the tractor rode over tussocks and rocks and then the rocky foreshore. I was not alone: three dogs and two suitcases crowded me against the trailer's edge. I was happy. I thought: this is a perfect place, this bumping of a trailer, these dogs, the secure outline of Conniach's back, all the safety of a crofter's skilled hands steering a tractor for me.

As the tractor stopped at the edge of the tideline's wet sand, I jumped down and looked out to sea. Fifty yards away was the wooden boat, Uistean's back heaving at oars, rowing his way to shore. I kicked off my shoes, picked them up, grabbed my suitcases and walked out into the surf.

The beach was flat, the shallows stretched far out. I met the boat, flung my suitcases over the side and jumped in the bow.

"Hello."

"Hello Marianne," said Uistean.

"You know who I am."

"Marianne. Your mother told me."

"Mother saw me?" I was disappointed.

"She did."

"I crashed the car."

Uistean turned the boat on the oars and headed out into the surf, towards the island, the white house, the sheep at its door.

"And the outboard's conked out," he said.

The door of the white house was dilapidated, peeling. It led into a long, damp hallway.

I arrived at the door just as Ysobel opened it. Ysobel was unsteady on her feet, and reached out to the door frame to keep her balance. Her voice was slurred.

"Hello, hello Marianne, sweetheart."

"You're drunk," I said.

"Am I? I suppose I am."

"Where's George?"

"Dead," said Ysobel.

"What?"

"You know, you know. Dead for years. Waist down. Neck up. I'm not sure which it is."

Ysobel turned and began to make her way down the hall. Calling as she went deeper into the house:

"Come in then. Where are your things? Did our delicious fisherman meet you? "

"I've stopped drinking," I called out to my mother's retreating back. "I've stopped, you see." I think that I wanted her to be pleased.

"Of course, of course. So has George."

In the grasses, among the rocks, on the land above the tideline, George was lying on his back. Squinting at the sky, he waved his hooded microphone at the end of an outstretched arm. Prone and straining and ridiculous.

Above him the adult shelduck were circling, calling in alarm, berating this intruder. Through the headphones these cries were piercing and frantic.

In the kitchen of the large white house, Ysobel was pouring drinks for us. Goblets of white wine. I sat at the table eating bread — just bread, no butter, no cheese — though they stood there in old dishes (the butter smeared with jam, the cheese patched with mould). In the distance the Connie Francis record had stuck — "Stupid Cupid you're a real . . . Stupid Cupid you're a real . . . Stupid Cupid you're a real . . ."

Without looking up, between mouthfuls of bread, I said, "For God's sake, mother."

Ysobel stamped her foot on the ground with startling force. The needle on the record skidded with a scratching noise, and the record player turned itself off.

"You know I hate you calling me mother."

"Because you're not a mother?"

"Because I'm not *only* a mother. If you call me Ma or Didi I don't feel such a prisoner."

"No one ever called you Didi!"

"Nom de plume. A writer's identity."

"But you're always telling us that you're glad you never really managed to be a writer."

"Exactly."

Ysobel laughed and poured herself another drink. She picked up the second glass and offered it to me.

"Are you sure?"

"Yes," I said. "Sure."

"Ah well."

And Ysobel put the full glass beside her own.

"I've stopped." I felt a sudden need to persuade my mother of at least this one fact.

"Have you now?"

George was crawling through the grasses of one of the island's headlands. Coarse grass on a ground of stones and tussocks. He crawled with headphones on, microphone raised aloft. He crawled with great discomfort.

Through the headphones, George heard the buffeting wind, the bumps of his heavy body on the ground, the gulps of his breath, and the occasional grunt of pain. His own sounds.

I walked along the beach. I bent to pick up shells, looked at them, held a large one to an ear, listening to the sea within. I could hear its hoarse breath. I looked up at the oyster catchers and gulls shrieking overhead. I found a nest of four rich brown eggs in the shingle. I stepped carefully past it. I looked out to sea.

I watched a boat lying among the surf and weeds beside barely submerged rocks. I realized it was the boatman, Uistean. He was standing in the boat's bow, hauling and setting lobster pots. He was tanned, lean — and young. Younger than me. I turned and walked away over the headland.

In the grass George pointed his microphone, as if aiming some powerful weapon. Through the headphones he heard the crunching of footsteps, the lapping of the sea on the beach, and the mewing of gulls. In the far distance a rumble, which turned into a roar exploding into his head. George tore off the headphones and tried to shield his ears from the noise.

On the boat Uistean took a lobster from a wicker trap, threw it onto the boards, and began to reset the trap with a chunk of dead fish.

A fire burned in the study of the big house. Driftwood logs were piled on both sides of the hearth: strange, bleached shapes. At a wide, oak table George was busy. The sections of his microphone, tape heads, cassettes and wires were laid out on one side; on the other were the barrel, stock and cleaning rods of a 12-gauge shotgun. He had spread out cans of cleaning fluid. Screwdrivers. Rags. A bright yellow duster. But everything neatly arranged.

He held a little patch of white linen. He squirted oil onto it. He wrapped the linen patch onto a metal mount. He screwed the mount to a rod. Then screwed this to a second rod. He picked up the gun barrel and thrust the rod into it, rubbing the fabric backwards and forwards, backwards and forwards, polishing the inside of the barrel.

Ysobel was lying on a faded chaise longue at the side of the room. Beside her was a small table with books, notepaper, a jar of pencils and a wine glass. Her eyes were closed — but she was not asleep.

I came into the room and walked over to the fire. I stood with my back to it, warming myself. I stared at the room. I squatted down to adjust the fire, taking trouble to balance another large and strangely twisted piece of driftwood in the flames. I stood up again, the fire hot against my back, and looked across the room at George. He had begun to rub the gun — barrel, stock, everything — with oil. And I looked at Ysobel, whose eyes remained closed.

"Your mother has not managed dinner, I'm afraid," said George. "And, er, neither have I. Sorry." I said nothing. There was a long silence. Then George said: "There's bread, cheese, cold bits and pieces. We can get them in a minute." He rubbed more oil into his gun. "I'll have this done and off the table."

"I don't need to eat, not just now," I said.

"A drink, then?"

"No thanks, George."

"Ah."

"Mother told me."

"Told you?"

"That you'd stopped drinking."

"Ah. Yes."

"So have I."

George reassembled his gun, pointed it at the light and peered down the barrel. Then he closed the breech with a metallic snap, wiped the stock, and took it over to a gun cupboard mounted on the wall. A box of cartridges was perched beside the gun rack.

Ysobel on the chaise longue opened her eyes and said:

"George, you're so fucking English. And so *male*."

I went to the table where George had been working and sat down. Looking at Ysobel, avoiding my eyes, George said, "Am I?"

Ysobel said, "Yes you are."

"Please . . . " I said.

"Don't worry dear. Your stepfather and I no longer have rows." Ysobel burst into words. "Since he stopped drinking he screams in silence. Great thing, sobriety. Leaves him free for other warfare. All very internal. Superior pauses. Wisely chosen remarks. The insightful shrug. Making sure that we all know who is the wicked one. It's all goodies and baddies in the house these days. Sort of male versus female. Women and men. Only nothing's quite as clear as it might be. Right George?"

George shrugged, and raised his eyebrows at me. Ysobel added, "See what I mean?"

Having finished with his gun, George picked up a large wooden box from under the table and tidied his recording equipment into its various compartments. He got up, gathered the box into his arms, and headed for the door. I opened the door for him. "Thanks Marianne," he said.

"That's his new version of storming out of the room," said Ysobel. "But he hasn't gone to sulk, or to walk off into the night. Oh no! He'll be back in a minute. With bread and cheese and some little snacky treat."

Silence again. Ysobel closed her eyes. I sat down at the table, then said:

"I like George. But then I never had a father."

Silence, broken by Ysobel:

"I don't know why you come to visit us."

"I don't visit you. Remember?"

"Of course. So why now? To tell us about your sobriety. Am I to have two angels in the house?"

I laughed. Ysobel smiled.

"What does George keep a shotgun for?"

"Menace," said Ysobel. "He needs to exude a sense of menace. All men do, don't they? Uncontrollable as well as unpredictable. That's where the power comes from. Isn't that what little boys' guns are all about? Like the bombers. Push a man too far and he'll rush to his cupboard and bang bang, silence at last. A warning in a cupboard on the wall."

I laughed and asked:

"Who's the boy in the boat?"

"Ahhh," said Ysobel. "The thin fisherman. The brown delight. Our jewel on the sea. Uistean." She paused, then went on: "Listen to the sea, my dear. Listen. And the wind."

Outside the windows of this room was the pale darkness of summer night. The glowing water shifted like quicksilver. The line of the beach half white surf, half the blackness of the tide flats.

"He's Conniach's boy," said Ysobel. "Conniach's the man who rescued you on the road. Ah, you shouldn't have stayed away from us so long. Our island is growing. Taller and stronger!"

The words seemed to be spoken in an enclosed and distant place. As if spoken from behind me, while in front of my eyes was the rolling of the waves on the land's edge. A gull's call in the night. My mind's eye followed this edge, travelling the foam's borders, the sighing of the sand, the grinding of shells, the making and wearing of the world.

Under the foam's sound, beyond the cry of a seabird in the night, the study door opened. A tray clattered. George came in.

"I've managed to pull together a bit of a supper. And a bottle of champagne. We can break our new habits and celebrate! After all, Marianne's back."

In a wide and thickly quilted bed, George caressed Ysobel. She lay very still, unresponding. George fingered her cheek, her lips, her teeth. He bent and kissed her. His tongue alongside his finger, touching and licking her lip, her mouth. With his other hand George pushed back the quilt, and tugged Ysobel's nightdress over her shoulder. He reached in to find her breast. He bent and licked the nipple. Touched the nipple. Licked again alongside his finger. He whispered into her body.

"Be a woman, Ysobel. You *are* a woman."

"I'm a drunk woman."

She reached down and stroked George's hair, pushing his head into her breasts. She reached under his chin. George whispered her name, "Ysobel . . . Ysobel . . . "

She pulled his head up to hers, put out her tongue, and pulled his mouth onto it, then pushed his head back again. "Ysobel."

Ysobel said, "George."

"Mm?"

"From behind."

She pushed George up and turned herself over underneath him, head on one side in the pillows, saying: "There's vaseline by your light switch."

The farm kitchen of the island house was cluttered with rows of gleaming old china on a dresser. Fish knives, ladles and wooden spoons hanging in lines like tools in a workshop. Saucepans of all sorts and sizes on high shelves. Jugs and bowls. Vases. Candlesticks. Even bookcases loaded with books. And a huge old black range in which a coal fire was burning. Old letters and newspapers were heaped on a pine table, with just enough space for three place settings: egg cups and spoons and side plates.

George was making toast in a round, mesh toaster set on the hot metal of the range. He had a dishcloth laid over one arm.

I was opening and shutting cupboards, looking for tea. George said:
"This is the farthest anyone got. The edge. Beyond the edge. Beyond order. The real milk's in the cow. There's powdered stuff in a packet up there somewhere."

I stared at him. "What are you talking about?"

"What? Powdered milk." said George.

"You were talking about order, the edge of something."

"The Romans. The boundaries of an empire."

"Oh."

George took a kettle off the stove and poured water into a teapot. I threw in the tea bags. George poured more water into a saucepan where he had already put two brown eggs. He turned over an hour-glass timer, sat down and watched the sand flow. "Exactly four and a half minutes," he said. "I time it."

He lifted an egg out of the water and set it in my egg cup. Another into his. He buttered four pieces of toast, then offered the salt.

"But the Romans didn't come this far north, did they?" I asked through a mouthful.

"A line of forts. Deals with tribal chiefs. All sorts of stuff keeps turning up here. Cut stones. Coins. Pots. Why wouldn't they come here?"

"Too many barbarians," I said.

"Hah!"

George carefully peeled the shell from the top of his boiled egg, then picked up his knife and cut off the white, ate it, laid down his knife, picked up a pinch of salt and sprinkled it on the exposed yolk, did the same with a pinch of pepper, picked up his spoon and took a first taste. I watched the precision of all these movements.

"Conniach'll be bringing the teaser tupp today," said George.

"Teaser tupp?"

George continued eating his egg. I tried copying his way of doing it.

"Never heard of a teaser tupp? Have to get all the ewes to lamb at the right time. So have to get them on heat, you know. No rams on the island these days. So they bring over a castrated tupp — he charges about the place, and the ewes all come into season. Then they whisk off the teaser and bring on the real thing. All the ewes get their man at about the same time, and bingo, the lambs are all born within a few days of one another."

"Wow!"

The sun shone hard and hot on the sands of a tight little cove hidden among the rocks of the island's shore. Steep sided, hidden, a sun trap. The sea rolled through weedbeds and over the sand of a shallow beach.

Naked, I ran down the beach. Running fast into the sea. Flailing and kicking against the cold. Then I swam into the weed, tangled up in it, shouted with delight as I stood, weed draped over my shoulders. I plunged through it, towards the clear water over the sand. I swam right into the shallows, then pulled myself by the hands, clawing my way through the surf, onto the beach. I sprawled at the surf line, nudged out of the water by the sea's rhythm. For a while I lay there, pushed and pulled, floated and dropped by the waves. I listened to the hiss of pebbles and shells coming and going, rising and falling in the sea's soft force. Then I crawled farther, beyond the surf's edge, got up and walked to where the sand was hot from the sun, and where my clothes had fallen in a pile beside a large beach towel. I lay on the towel, then rolled myself up in it until, on my back and covered, eyes closed, I soaked in the rays of the sun.

In the distance was the sound of an outboard motor. Uistean's boat, lobster pots piled on the deck, puttered across the mouth of the bay. Uistean, watching the bow of his boat, didn't even glance towards the beach where I lay. I turned my head and watched the boat go by.

An old chapel, roof gone, caught the sun on its walls. The broken stone a hard shadow of what was once there. Around it a jumble of old graves, some of them marked with high Celtic crosses. Other Celtic remains rested against the chapel walls. Nettles rose as high as the gravestones, sheep grazed in the chapel doorway.

Beyond the chapel was a grassy bank. Gorse bushes and pale rock broke the ground's surface; the earth's skeleton. At the top of the bank, over the ridge, the horizon: sky and sea.

I came into this horizon with Ysobel; our two figures looming from the hidden side of the bank. We were walking towards the chapel. Ysobel was wearing a long, cotton dress, a head scarf, and dark glasses. I was wearing old walking boots, cut-off jeans and no top. My beach towel was round my shoulders, a sort of cumbersome college scarf. My hair was wet.

We clambered down the bank, picked our way by nettles and gorse, walked into the chapel ruins. The sun was shining into the old doorway. I walked into the sunlight and raised my towel over my head, stretching it between my arms like a cloth banner, opening myself to the sun. I said to Ysobel:

"I always had the feeling this was some kind of nunnery and the ghosts are irrational."

"Probably with habits," said Ysobel.

"Ghosts and spirits and . . . and women. That's what's here."

"George will tell you that this is an early Christian church," said Ysobel. "Built five hundred years after the fall of the Roman empire. Built by Christianity — the religion the Romans left behind them. Not much to do with the barbarians and their spirits."

"You know what I mean, though."

"Poor George is obsessed by the Romans."

"More interesting," I said, "than recording the wind and the birds."

"I wonder," said Ysobel.

I draped the towel round my shoulders. The two of us walked

through the gravestones and up onto the headland. I turned to Ysobel:

"Listen, I want to have things out with you. I mean, there are things I need to know. About what happened. About who I am. And you. Why do we never see each other?"

"I'd find it easier to talk to you if you had more clothes on."

"For God's sake. I'm your daughter. We're both women."

She said: "Perhaps that's why I'd expect us to talk with our clothes *on.*"

The sound of a boat reached us from behind the rocks below the headland. "I think it's the teaser tupp," said Ysobel.

"Where?"

"Coming round now."

Uistean was steering his outboard engine, nudging his way along the shallows, heading for the jetty below the chapel. A second, larger boat appeared: it was Conniach. In the bow were two sheep-dogs and the castrated ram. Behind the boat five bullocks were being towed to shore.

"Tupp for sheep. And cattle to eat the long grass," said Ysobel.

Uistean jumped ashore from his boat, and tied it to a buoy lying on the beach. He turned back into the water to help with Conniach's boat. As it grounded in the sand, he reached in, hauled out the tupp and chased it up the beach onto the grass beyond.

George ran through the grass, pulling the headphones from his ears, swearing under his breath, and disappeared into the white house. Two F11 fighter bombers swept in at the sea, a steeple's height above the grey-green waves. They were silent, their vapour trails curving behind them, looming towards the island.

George came charging out of the house with his shotgun and a box of cartridges. He dropped the box on the ground, thrust two cartridges in the breech, and snapped it shut.

The bombers were overhead. George aimed at them, fired both barrels, reloaded, and fired again. The sound of the third and fourth shots was drowned by the roar of the planes' engines. George fired a last two shots at their tails as they swept away from the island, and screamed after them:

"The goddamned shit-heaping bastards! They think it's a fucking game. Fuck off! Go and wank in the mess hall!"

We were startled by the shots. We walked towards the house. I wrapped the towel around me. No nakedness now. Ysobel called out: "George, George."

They watched the plane disappear. The sheep also looked up at the noise. Urged and pulled by Uistean and Conniach, the cattle were pushing their way ashore, the sheep-dogs barking at their heels. Uistean and Conniach were talking to each other in Gaelic.

In the house, George took his gun apart at the study table. His cleaning tools were again spread out in front of him. On one side stood the box in which he carried the recording equipment and accessories. Ysobel was lying on the chaise longue. I was arranging driftwood on the fire. I stood up and turned to warm my back.

"I think we should go to the wall," said George.

"What?"

"The Roman wall," answered George. "An outing."

"You really do care about it, don't you?" I said.

"The largest monument the Romans left." George's voice was full of sudden energy. "Perhaps the largest manmade object in Europe. A superb symbol — of engineering genius, the nature of civilization. Also remarkably beautiful. Also, a myth. Real and unreal."

"Obsessed," said Ysobel.

"Am I? Yes. But think of it: the collaborators. All of *us*, the English have collaborated. We're *proud* of the Romans, as if they're our ancestors, as if they are us — but they're the *invaders*, the foreigners who came and turned us into slaves. Slaves to their ideas about the world. But good ideas. That's the trouble. The best ideas. Ideals — of life, stone, manhood."

George, reassembling the shotgun, said: "We could all go tomorrow."

"Mother would never go," I said.

"Uistean can take us," answered George.

Uistean steered the boat through reefs and beds of seaweed, keeping to the channel that led to the mainland. He was concentrating on this job, full of a quiet self-importance, making a simple task appear full of difficulty.

On the boat's central bench sat Ysobel and George, facing forwards. They were wearing their best clothes: George had a tweed jacket and flat cap, Ysobel a large black shawl spread over a woollen jacket.

I was in the bow, leaning back, facing Uistean. I was watching him. He looked up from his scanning of the sea and caught my eye. And smiled. I think I gave a quick smile, and looked away.

Uistean was driving the Land Rover along the Roman road beside the wall. Ysobel sat in the front, next to Uistean. George and I were in the back. George was trying to read a map. I stared along the road that stretched dead straight behind us, up and down the Northumberland hills. Ysobel held a hip flask in her lap. Uistean had his hand on the long gear stick that almost pressed against Ysobel's knee.

Ysobel turned to George and me and waved her flask at us. This caused her to lean hard against Uistean. George shook his head. I turned and looked at Uistean, catching his eye in the driving mirror. He winked. I turned away, looked back at the road.

The Land Rover pulled into a carpark by the wall and juddered to a halt. No one got out. George said: "I wonder how long we'll be. You could pick us up at the pub along the road. Say three o'clock."

"I'm sure Uistean would be fascinated by the wall," said Ysobel, and laid a hand on his arm. "You must come with us. You can represent the invaders from the north."

George began: "I expect Uistean would prefer to visit . . . "

"Uistean, are you with us or waiting for us?" asked Ysobel.

Uistean said, "I'm with you."

I jumped out of the back of the Land Rover. George was watching me. I turned, saw George, and held out my hand in a parody of courtesy. "May I?"

In the front I saw Ysobel rest her hand on Uistean's leg. I thought: she's going to give his genitals a quick squeeze. She seemed to pout in a deliberate parody of lust. I heard — could I have heard? — her fake moan "Ooo . . . *uh*!"

The wall climbed over a steep crag on its march across the land. Beside the wall was a little, switchbacking path. In places a series of precipitous and slippery stones were set steplike into the bank. Uistean, carrying a picnic basket, helped me up the highest, steepest section of the path. He caught my hand and pulled me towards him. I felt the firmness of his hold on me, the strength of the tug that jerked me to the top.

Farther along the track, Ysobel and George were separately making their way to the easier section lower down.

I disappeared over the ridge. Uistean stood at the peak, waiting for George and Ysobel, proud in his readiness to help them.

I clambered up onto the wall itself. I stood looking across vast sweeps of countryside. I heard the lilt of a Gaelic song and looked around me, puzzled. The song grew a little louder, though carried and hidden by the wind. I walked nervously to the very edge of the wall and peered over. There was Uistean leaning against the bottom of it, singing. He was looking up. When he saw me see him he laughed and called out: "Barbarian invader."

"It sounded great," I said. "Let's hear some more."

"Just look at yon land to the north." Uistean exaggerated his accent. "Can ye imagine it? Highland kings and the wild of it."

George and I walked side by side along the wall where it passed through a stand of pines. George said:

"The edge of the empire. The limits. Beyond . . . *terra incognita*, the unknown. Not just unknown. Irrational. That's the magic of the place. A limit. The Romans knew, defined their limits."

I said: "But isn't it all bullshit?"

George turned his head to stare at me, disapproving, spluttering, "You what?"

"The Romans. Isn't it all a myth, I mean, stories we've made up to justify modern life. Nineteenth-century invention of our proper ancestors. Making sure we aren't descendants of the wild tribes. Isn't that what you said to me?"

"No. It was the nineteenth-century scholars who realized what was hidden under the stones, if you know what I mean," said George.

"But on the other side of their frontiers." I wanted to argue with him. "The people who weren't conquered. Or not yet, anyway. The barbarians. The Picts. Who were they? No one ever talks about them."

"No one knows a thing about them. Those Victorian scholars weren't interested."

"I bet they couldn't cope with all those spirits and ghosts and the irrational."

"Perhaps," said George. "Perhaps."

I walked beside the battlements of a section of the wall that had been rebuilt. Farther along, at the doorway to the upper level of a reconstructed mile castle, Uistean was again lilting a Gaelic air. I stopped, and looked over the edge. The wall and then a bank fell away beneath me, a drop of at least thirty feet. I whistled in amazement.

In the courtyard beside the wall and mile castle, George and Ysobel were looking at a gigantic ancient crossbow, its massive arrow aimed at the hills to the north. George, thumbing through a guidebook, said:

"I hope he can keep his hands off Marianne."

"Don't be revolting," said Ysobel.

George began to read from the guidebook: "From time to time the barbarians managed to overrun the wall. In 184 and again in 273. Causing great damage."

"And did the Romans defend their lines?" asked Ysobel.

"No, my dear. Not their style. They sent crack troops out. They fought back where they fought best. I'm sure the slaughter was wondrous to behold."

"Vengeance," said Ysobel.

"Pre-emptive vengeance," said George. "In the long run. Slow accumulations, sudden explosions, violent warning, lasting peace. *Modus operandi Romanis*. Limits at the edge of empire. Tight reins. Bursts. A ripping of the tissue."

George was trembling. He closed the book and stuffed it back in a pocket. He reached out to Ysobel, clutching her arm, pleading with her: "Ysobel, for God's sake."

In the background, the sound of Uistean's singing had become muffled. He must have gone into the mile castle.

Ysobel hurried up the wooden steps of the mile castle, making her way from ground to upper level. I could see her, distant but clear. Uistean's singing, loud at first, stopped. He was waiting for her at the top of the steps, in the gloom of a small, stone-walled room. The only light came through a door leading out onto the battlements.

Ysobel caught hold of Uistean's arm and led him into a corner of the room. Even there, in the dark, I could see her. Distant, glowing. She stood close to him. She took hold of the lapels of his jacket, and pulled him against her. She leaned her head on his and licked his ear. As she licked she whispered to him, spacing the words:

"Keep . . . your . . . fucking . . . hands . . . off . . . Marianne."

She pulled back and looked him straight in the eye. I heard her say: "Anyway, she's a lesbian."

Uistean put his arms round Ysobel's lower back. He moved a hand over her buttocks. Ysobel murmured to him, "Jesus Christ, you make me drip."

Uistean found the hip flask in Ysobel's pocket, pulled it out, unscrewed the cap and raised it to Ysobel's mouth, feeding her.

I walked with Ysobel among the ruins of a Roman fortress: the outlines of residences, granary, married quarters and a central well were all labelled with British Tourist Trust signs.

"Why don't you leave the island?" I asked Ysobel. "You could live . . . anywhere. Have friends. You're so cut off. What happens, I mean, if something happens? You used to have friends. You used to write. What happened to you? And how do you live? I mean, money. Does George ever earn anything? Do you?"

"George has an army pension," said Ysobel. "He's a war hero, remember."

"So you could move. Wouldn't George want to?"

"I wouldn't want to." Ysobel's voice was suddenly childlike. "I belong at the edge. With the Roman army! I may not write, but I'm a writer. My image of myself. Anyway, we couldn't afford to live anywhere else. Realism dictates."

"You could sell the place," I said. "For a fortune. It's a jewel."

"Private income. I couldn't. We must remember our origins."

"You're drunk. Already."

"A reason — George's reason — for staying on the island. My drunkenness is what keeps us there. We should all be grateful! What's that noise?"

I said, "It sounds like someone being sick." We looked around to see where the noise was coming from.

The Land Rover was in a carpark by the Roman camp remains. Uistean was leaning against the driver's door. George was holding onto a branch a few yards away. He was vomiting into the hedge.

Ysobel hurried over to George, who spat and spluttered. "Those shrimp sandwiches," he said. "And we have to hurry. Uistean says we might miss the tide."

The long, flat beach of a falling tide. Shallow rock and sand pools. Splatterings of seaweed. Wading birds dashing about, feeding. Midway between tideline and surf Uistean dragged and I pushed the boat across the sand. Ysobel, walking ahead, stopped for us to reach her and then grasped the rope and helped Uistean pull. George was carrying the picnic basket and our shoes. We were all barefoot.

The boat reached the surf. Uistean steadied it, letting Ysobel jump into the bow. He pushed the boat to deeper water. I waded out and jumped into the stern. Uistean turned the boat sideways to the surf and nudged it as far back to the shore as he dared, waiting for George. George flung the picnic basket and shoes aboard and then grappled with the boat's edge. Uistean moved round to help him.

"I'm alright," said George. "I'm alright." And he clambered into the middle seat. Uistean, thigh deep in the sea, pushed the boat farther. With a last push he levered himself on board, grabbed an oar and poled the boat into the waves. Ten yards out he dropped the oar, caught me by the shoulder, and moved me to the seat beside George. Uistean settled into the stern seat and lowered the outboard into the water. The boat bobbed and turned in the waves.

"I'll row," I said.

Uistean wound the starting cord on the outboard and tugged. The engine refused to fire. I manoeuvred the oars into the rowlocks. George had to climb out of the way, joining Ysobel in the bow. Uistean pulled again. The engine wouldn't fire. I made my first stroke. Still nothing from the engine. I rowed. Uistean pulled the cord, the engine fired, and the boat lurched forwards. I lifted first one and then the other oar into the boat.

The boat surged out towards the island. George and Ysobel crouched in the bow, facing forwards. Uistean and I looked at one another's eyes, laughing.

I sat against an inside stone wall of the ruined chapel, sheltering from the wind, feeling the sun. I was reading. A book about the Roman wall. I closed my eyes and lay my head back on the stone. I let one hand fall between my legs.

The sun was red and orange through my eyelids. I turned my head to one side.

In my mind's eye, Uistean reached down and lifted my hand from my legs and gently stroked my arm. I sighed to myself and turned my head back to the sun. The orange blazed in my eyes. I turned away again. Now in my mind's eye: Uistean is stroking my bare arm. He bends down and runs his cheek along it, turning his head as he does so to bite the skin — gently, no more than holding the flesh between his teeth for a moment. I turn my face up to the sun, my eyelids fill again with red and orange. Into this colour comes a face of the Roman wall: the texture and pattern of the stones flowing along, flowing through the sunlight, through my mind. And a glimpse of turrets. Walls, so many walls, and then, suddenly, at last, through them to the hills and heather far beyond.

The sound of dogs barking broke into the fantasy. I opened my eyes. Uistean was there with Conniach's two dogs. I was embarrassed. Uistean looked at me and said, "You're reading."

"That's alright."

Uistean stared at me, giving his whole attention, flirting, saying: "I like to come here. I think it's full of spirits. Don't you?"

"Yes," I answered. "In a way . . . "

"I'm looking for the ram."

"Why?"

"Time to take him home."

"The job's done!" I laughed. "Can I help? Watch the dogs or something?"

"Marianne . . . "

I interrupted him and looked away, saying, "Let's go and find that ram of yours."

Uistean and I walked along a grassy headland. Uistean was whistling to the dogs. I stopped.

"Look!" I said. "Over there. The islands. Like the bones of the sea. The islands hold the world together. That's what the Romans didn't understand."

"The Romans?"

"My stepfather is obsessed by the Romans. You must have noticed the other day. The shrimp picnic! He's persuaded me to read about the wall."

Behind us the sea was flat, glistening, broken by rocky islets and, farther off, black humps of land.

"What did you think of it?"

"The wall?" said Uistean. "I liked being there with you. I mean, you made me think about the stones."

"The stones?"

"Look, there's the old boy!" And he whistled, then called, to the dogs. "Hup! Hup! Heyoo-oo!"

The dogs sped along the headland. Sheep scrambled up the bank ahead of them. Among them the ram. The dogs were barking; the sheep were bleating. Suddenly Uistean exclaimed: "Hey, what the . . ." George had leapt up from the grass. He was waving his microphone and screaming. He was still wearing his headphones. He shrieked:

"Get these fucking dogs out of here. Get them off!"

Through his headphones George could hear the dogs and sheep — distorted and deafening. He could also hear me laughing. Then all these noises were drowned out by the roar of a low-flying jet. Uistean and I pressed our hands against our ears. George tore off his headphones and dropped to his knees. There, on the ground, was a picnic basket and his shotgun. He grabbed the gun and fired two shots at the plane. As the plane's roars began to fade, George reloaded and was about to fire again. I shouted at him: "George, stop it! Stop it! You're crazy!"

Uistean said, "Those planes are way out of range of a shotgun."

"Then why do it?"

"Someone has to do it, don't they? What else could he do? To stop the planes, I mean." Uistean leant close to me and said into my ear: "And to think that I was just about to kiss you." But I turned away, looking over the headland, watching the plane's spreading vapour trail. George had walked up the headland, as if hoping to get within range of the jet after all.

"Well," said Uistean. "I'd better gather up the sheep." He called again to the dogs. "It'll be hot work. We can have a swim. I'll shut the ram in the boat."

"I'll go and see if George is OK."

Uistean walked away, towards the dogs and the sheep. He called back over his shoulder: "The beach below the chapel."

I stared at him as he walked.

George knelt in the grass, the gun and headphones on the ground beside him. His eyes were closed and he was shaking, sobbing. Seeming to repress, but revealing, a crazed misery. I was kneeling beside him.

"George. What . . . ? I don't understand."

George shuddered.

"You know, I think you and Mum should get away from the island."

George's sobs grew louder, coming from deep inside him.

I put my arms round him. "George. George. What is it?"

"I can't bear him." The words came in jerks, through the tears. "I just can't bear him."

At the beach where I swam before, Uistean lay face down on the rocks. He was wearing his jeans. Bare back; bare feet. I sat beside him, fully dressed, arms around my legs, head resting on my knees.

"Where do you live?" asked Uistean.

"I . . . I don't know. Why do you live here?"

"I was born here. At least, over there on the mainland. What do you mean, you don't know where you live?"

"I think I was born in London."

"I thought you came from here. Or somewhere in the Highlands. I mean, your mother's always been here."

" No, no. This is the retirement home. It's just that they returned very young!"

I struggled to remember obvious facts. The island, the beach, this man — they seemed to be so far away from me, and yet they contained me, and cut me off from a simpler, factual world.

"And your home?"

"I don't know. London, I suppose. But something's happening. I feel . . . I feel that something's gone wrong. Perhaps it's the sun. The sea. I don't know. Nothing seems to exist. I mean, nothing *else*. No past. A nonperson. Nonwoman. Nonman."

"Your mother says she doesn't know anything about you."

"How do you know what she knows?"

"Well, I asked her about you."

There was silence between us. Then I said, "Why don't you swim?"

"Why don't you?"

"I'm shy."

"I'm not." Uistean stood up, turned round, took off his jeans and walked towards the sea. At the edge of the water he turned to face me. "Come on!" He stepped backwards into the water. Stepped again. The water was at his knees. He tripped, fell in, rolled over, and doggy-paddled into the waves.

I stood up.

A storm beat against the windows of George and Ysobel's bedroom. A heavy velvet curtain filled and emptied with the drafts. A bedside light was on. George lay next to the light, on his back, eyes open, tense, staring.

I stood at the window of my bedroom. I was wearing a nightgown. I was listening to the wind and rain. Surf boomed on the beach below. I opened the window. The sounds and wet swept into the room. I let myself be buffeted then closed the window, picked up a flashlight, and went out of the room.

At the doorway to the white house I pulled on an oilskin coat, gumboots and a sou'wester. I clutched the coat around me.

I walked along the shore. The breakers crashed; the foam rushed at me. I walked out into the sea. Into the waves. Water surged from my knees to my waist.

I walked along the line of the surf. I reached the jetty, and clambered onto it. In the lee of the jetty, the sea was calm. I flashed my torch out onto the water. I lit up the mooring buoys rolling with the sea. Then I heard a strange thumping and groaning sound. Very close to me. I discovered two ropes tied to mooring rings set in the stone. I peered over the jetty's lee side, following the line of the ropes, and saw a dinghy. Protective rubber tires on the dinghy's side were thumping against the jetty.

I left the jetty and walked along the shingle of the beach. Turning my face away from the force of the wind and rain, I noticed a flicker of light. It was gone. No, it flickered again. I could just make out the profile of the boathouse.

I made my way to the boathouse door. I shone my torch, moving the beam across it, searching for a handle. I noticed a piece of string hanging from a latch slot, reached out, and pulled. Nothing happened. I pulled harder. There was a clank, and the door opened towards me. A candle light guttered in the gusts from the open door, and went out. The door, caught by the wind, thumped into me. I tried to hold it but couldn't. It blew wide open. In the beam of my torch I saw Uistean on his back, Ysobel astride him. Patches of them in the dim light. Ysobel, eyes closed, was moaning, shouting.

Uistean called out. "Who's that? Ysobel, there's a light."

But I switched off the light, turned and stumbled away.

I rushed along the jetty, the rain slashing at me. Face and hair soaked; water dripping down me, off me. I was panting, gasping, weeping. I was frozen to the core of my being.

I reached the boat and grabbed the rope tied to the mooring ring. I grappled with it, untied it. I pulled at the boat, hauling it up against the jetty, and let go, leaving it crash into the waves. I pulled again, and again, and again. My arms ached, my strength was insufficient. I flung down the rope and left the boat to batter and drift. I turned back towards the house.

Inside the house, I stumbled along the corridor. It was dark. I guided myself by the wedge of light reaching the corridor from a slightly open door. I went to that door. It was Ysobel and George's bedroom. George was there, bedside light on. He was not asleep but lay staring, with a book about the Roman wall open on his chest. One hand held the book, the other flopped beside the bed. His eyes were swollen, his cheeks tear stained. I moved to the bedside, looked at him, and began shaking and pummelling him. He stared at me.

"George, wake up. Wake up! They're in the boathouse. They're in the fucking boathouse. Yes, fucking. Jesus, George. *Do* something. Go and *do* something."

I was almost lying on him, punching his shoulders.

"Please, George."

George pushed me to one side. He was shaking. He stepped out of bed. He was wearing tattered pajamas.

In his study, George took his shotgun from the gun cupboard and picked up a handful of cartridges. He was still shaking. He grabbed his coat.

Barefoot, in pajamas and coat, shotgun in one hand, flashlight in another, George made his way through the rain to the boathouse. I stood by the front door. The white shape of the house seemed to be uncertain, ghostlike. A lamp lit the doorway and the grass slope in front of me. I felt as if the blood had gone from my body. I imagined I was as pale as mist. I stared at George's rainswept, disappearing figure. I wanted to stay there, in a pool of lamplight. I wanted to follow him.

In the boathouse, Uistean, covered only in a blanket, was lighting a line of candles set on the blade of an old oar. Lobster pots, fuel cans, coils of rope, trolling lines, old buoys, net floats, boxes of engine parts: a great muddle of boating and fishing gear was piled all around. In the empty space beside Uistean were more blankets and an eiderdown. He heard the click of the door catch. But it was locked. Someone pushed at it hard. "Ysobel?" said Uistean.

The catch broke. The door swung open. Uistean saw George in the doorway, shotgun in hand. He stared at him, terrified.

George walked in, pointing the shotgun at Uistean. Uistean moved back. Watching. Crouching. "George."

George turned the gun and held it by the barrel, pointing at himself. "George," said Uistean. "Marianne . . . "

George swung the gun like an axe, shoulder height, fast and hard. The stock crunched into Uistean's neck. George swung again. Uistean rolled on the floor, squirming, writhing, grunting, whimpering. George swung and flailed. Some blows hit, others missed. The stock, as it swung, caught oars, boxes, buoys, junk. Caught the edges of a stack of lobster pots. Two wicker boxes fell onto the light of the candles. There was darkness, then the brightness of a flame, and the boathouse was burning.

George staggered out, backing away from the fire, still holding his gun by the barrel. His face was streaked with tears, dirt, soot. His hands and the gun were smeared with blood.

Ysobel and I were standing outside, staring. George saw us and stumbled past. Ysobel said, "He's gone mad."

"Uistean," I said. "Where's Uistean?"

Ysobel shrugged.

Burning timbers fell into the flames, and threw sparks into the night sky. At the edge of the boathouse, the coarse grass of the shoreline was burning. The white-capped waves of the rough sea flashed in the night;

light and darkness. The dinghy I had cut loose was drifting, half full of water, drifting and pitching and turning, lost in the dark.

Ysobel and I were in the kitchen. Wrapped in a dusty apron, I was making bread. White hands in the flour, squeezing and pressing the dough into shape. Four bread tins stood in the warmth of the range, with dough set to rise. I moulded the bread she had been kneading into a fifth tin and put it alongside the others. I clapped my hands to shed flour, wiped them on my apron, and went over to the table where Ysobel was sitting slicing vegetables. She was arranging them on a large chopping board: carrots, potatoes, onions, cauliflower. To her side was a bowl of beetroot and a grater.

I sat down across the table from Ysobel, picked up a beetroot and the grater, and began grating.

"Why are we doing this?" asked Ysobel.

"I'm a bread and borscht specialist," I said.

Ysobel chopped; I grated. "Farewell dinner," I said.

"George won't eat," said Ysobel.

Ysobel chopped; I grated. My hands were turning blood red. Ysobel looked at me, saying: "And you're not leaving."

"I am," I said.

"You can't. The boat's gone."

"Conniach'll come."

I swept beetroot into a large saucepan, took another beetroot from the bowl. Ysobel, very still, her knife held in a clenched fist, watched me. "You have to stay with me." She paused; I grated. "You and I, we belong . . . I mean, we are . . . well, flesh of my flesh. The two of us."

I said: "I don't know what you're talking about." I reached out, took a handful of vegetables, put them in the saucepan with the beetroot, then added more of the beetroot. My hands were bright red; where I wiped my brow and scratched my nose, smudges of beetroot juice had marked my face.

"What about George?" I asked.

"He's dead," said Ysobel.

"He's asleep," I said. "He'll eat with us."

"He's a clown." Ysobel snorted. "Some male principle dressed up with a false nose. Painted eyes."

I wiped my hands on my apron and went to the range where the bread was rising. I said: "But you married him."

"Age. Loneliness. His boyishness." Ysobel hesitated. "His maleness. I mean, order, all that. The principle. I need it. You can eat what you need. Or you can eat. "She laughed. "Who would have thought it?"

"Who was my father?" I asked. I thought: how many times have I asked this before?

"Your father? The bottle! A different principle!"

Ysobel went to a cupboard and began searching shelves. She collected up several old packets, discovered a head of garlic, and found a mortar and pestle. She brought these to the table and sat down. "I'll help with the flavour." She poured herbs and spices into the mortar, beginning to grind them.

I said: "What are we going to do?"

"Do?"

"About, about the fire. And . . . "

"No remains. Ash. A pile of ash."

"But his father," I said. "I mean, we must explain. Or something."

"Conniach came over this morning," said Ysobel. "You were asleep. He found the boat on the mainland. Washed up below the croft. Smashed, sunk, he said. And the boy: presumed drowned."

I froze, staring at this mother of mine.

Ysobel sniffed the mix in the mortar, set some aside on a saucer, and added the garlic.

"You don't feel a thing. You . . . you . . . screw up everyone, and . . . and . . . cook."

Ysobel tasted the contents of the mortar and sprinkled them over the vegetables in the pot, saying: "I'm you. In your old — well, your middle age." She peered into the pot. "The mixture has to be just right. No easy thing. I'm sorry, have I taken over your cooking?"

I stared and stared at her. Trying to *see* her. But I could find no thoughts. She silenced even the deepest, innermost voices.

"How's the bread doing?" she said. "We make a perfect team."

"You drunken bitch!" At last I could shout at her. "You murderous . . . Christ, you're awful. You make me feel . . . stifled, strangled. You use everyone to . . . And you sit there grinding herbs!"

"You're the bread and borscht expert," said Ysobel. "You're doing the cooking. Look at your hands." I looked at my blood-red hands. I said:

"I can't believe you're my mother. I can't believe it!"

"Marianne," said Ysobel. "You're driving me to drink."

"I'm getting out of here," I yelled. "I'm leaving this place."

"No you're not."

"There's no space here. I'm . . . I'm going."

"You're staying right here," said Ysobel. "As they say in the books, we're in this together."

At the same moment we both heard the distant drone of a helicopter. I jumped up and moved towards the door. Ysobel caught hold of my wrist and said with softness in her voice: "Wait, just wait. You've come back to me. Let's take the opportunity. I mean, let's work it out."

The helicopter was getting much louder. I tried to get out of Ysobel's grip, to look out of the window, to see what was making the noise. I said: "It's the police." And Ysobel let me go.

A military helicopter landed on the island, not far from the charred and sprawled remains of the boathouse. The blast from the blades caused ash at the fire's edge to swirl into the air. A uniformed military policeman jumped out. He was armed and carrying a briefcase. He headed towards the house. The helicopter engine came to a halt. The pilot climbed down. He was also in uniform, but not armed.

Ysobel and I walked towards the policeman. The pilot walked towards the remains of the boathouse. We watched in horror as he kicked at ashes and poked at a charred roof timber.

The policeman stood beside us. He followed our eyes, and saw that they were fixed on the pilot by the burned boathouse. "You had a fire?" he said.

"The boathouse," said Ysobel.

"Much damage?" asked the policeman.

"Damage?" Ysobel squinted at him.

"Much inside when it went up?"

Ysobel looked away, towards the pilot and the remains of the boathouse. Something in the ashes caught the pilot's eye. He squatted among the ashes to look. He reached out, pulled a timber to one side, trying to see something more clearly. Ysobel and the policeman watched. My eyes, too, were drawn into the charred wood and ashes. I heard myself say: "Tea. Let's have some tea."

The policeman said "Thanks," then noticed my hands, the smears on my face, and the stained clothes. I noticed him notice.

"Beetroot," I said. "Soup."

"Ah," said the policeman.

"Inside," I said. "The house. And your pilot?"

The policeman shouted: "Hey, Jeff. Tea?"

The pilot, Jeff, picked up a stick and poked at the ashes. They were still hot. He pushed the stick backwards and forwards. The end of the stick hit something hard. He used the stick to nudge whatever it was, then cleared ashes away to see what was there. He bent down and began to explore with great care. He called out to the others: "Hot! But hey, what's here?" He reached into the ashes. He stood up. "Look at this!"

And he walked over to the others. "Look," he said, showing them his hand full of charred coins.

"What are they?" I asked.

"They're Roman," said the pilot. He handed the coins towards me. I held out a blood-red hand and took them.

"Beetroot," I said.

"George's," said Ysobel. "My husband, he's a Roman enthusiast. He mostly used the boathouse." She turned to lead the way to the white house.

The policeman followed and asked: "Is your husband home?"

"I think so," said Ysobel.

We walked along the corridor of the house. As she passed George's study, Ysobel pushed its door open and looked in. No one was there. "George?" called Ysobel. "George!" She turned to the others. "I don't know where he is."

The policeman, standing at the door with Ysobel, suddenly said: "Perhaps I could ask you a couple of questions. In here?"

"Of course," said Ysobel, and led him into the study. He closed the door behind him. The two of them stood there, awkward.

"A drink?" said Ysobel.

"No thanks." The policeman hesitated. "Er, where do you think he is, your husband?"

"I don't know," said Ysobel. "On the island somewhere, I suppose. Looking for birds. He records birdsong, you know. His interest. That and the Romans."

"Does he have a gun?" asked the policeman.

"A gun?"

"A shotgun." The policeman was standing by the gun cupboard. "In here perhaps. Mind if I look?"

"Of course, said Ysobel. "Have a look."

He opened the cupboard and saw the gun rack and the cartridges. No gun, though. He reached out and picked up a cartridge. "Number four," he said.

"Number four?" Ysobel's voice was taut with fear.

"The size of the shot. About right for pigeons."

"Pigeons?"

"Let's not beat about the bush."

"For pigeons," said Ysobel, and smiled at him.

"This isn't a joke," he said, turned the number four cartridge over in his hand and looked again at the gun cupboard. "I expect this *is* the gun's home. It was a shotgun, I believe."

"I don't know what you're talking about," said Ysobel.

"We won't quarrel. When you find your husband, tell him that shooting at planes is not a bright idea. Dangerous."

"They're a long way out of range, aren't they? Of a shotgun?"

"Dangerous," said the policeman. "And illegal."

"I'll tell him."

The policeman and the pilot climbed back into their helicopter. The blast of wind from the blades raised another cloud of ashes from the boathouse.

George scraped with a trowel at the bottom of a trench he had dug in one of the island's grassy banks. He fingered soil on the trowel, searching every grain. He was unshaven and dirty. His face grey, his clothes torn and mud smeared, his fingernails blackened and broken.

I walked to the edge of the trench. I watched him for a moment. George looked up at me and continued digging, searching. Then he said, as if to the earth: "She must stay here. With us. She mustn't leave us now. She belongs."

I turned away from the trench rim. George scrabbled in the earth, muttering to himself. "I *know* they were here. Those coins. More coins. I'll find pots. Inscribed stones. *De civitate.* You'll keep her here, won't you? *In femino masculium. Ab initio.* Yes, yes. *Reductio ad absurdum.*" He chuckled into the ground.

I lay on my bed in my room in the white house. The window was open. From outside came the sounds of the sea and birds. Distant. I curled on my side, eyes closed. Beside the bed stood Ysobel. She said to me:

"I know you're not asleep. So I'll talk to you anyway. Keep your eyes closed if it helps." She waited for a reaction. I lay still, making even my breath into no more than the slightest movements. I wanted a perfect stillness. "Listen to me then." But she hesitated. "Life has not been as I had expected. As I'd hoped. *My* life, I mean, of my making." She sat near me, so near me, and reached out to stroke my hair, my cheek, my lips. Her hand was very cold. Not human, easily disregarded. I thought: if I don't move I shall feel nothing.

Ysobel said: "You could be beautiful. A woman." She ran her hand down my side, at the edge of my breast. I thought: if I stop breathing, I will feel nothing. I thought: she must not, she dare not, touch my breast. She said: "I was beautiful. But never a woman. I used to look at you, when you were a baby, as you grew, as you became a person, I used to look at you and feel it within me — as if *I* was growing at last, as if here was *my* chance. And I wanted, I so wanted, to be *you*. I *was* you. I went into your soul, filled out your shape with mine. Gave myself another time. Is that why we become parents? Even women who have never been female? Is that the immortality that parents try to find? Giving ourselves another *time.*" She touched my hand. "You were to be the woman for me. And you are. You are. We're one person. Now. At last. All of us. Yes, with George. You and George. The female and the male. The two of you give me life." She looked at me, then at the sky through the open window. "We're together. We killed the barbarian. We've turned him to smoke, to dust. We've converted him into island atmosphere! We've got rid of him, and made him part of ourselves. We can breathe him in! We shared his body — yes, George too! Now we can share his spirit. Him in us. Us in him." She held me with both hands, pressing me, hugging me." So you'll stay. You have to, you see. You're one of us. We're imprisoned."

I no longer wanted to be still. I turned round under Ysobel's hands and opened my eyes. Ysobel took my face between her hands and kissed me on the cheek, then the lips, and said: "You see. You see, don't you?" But I couldn't see because I couldn't feel. Only the coldness of her skin.

I slept on my bed, under the covers. I woke with a start. The room was dark. I looked around me, at the shapes of things. I sat up in bed. I was confused, frightened. I swung my legs over the side of the bed. I was dressed in jeans and sweater, barefoot. I stood up. I walked to the door, and grabbed the handle. I turned and pulled. The door wouldn't open. I pulled then shook the door. It was locked. I tried again, incredulous. I banged the door. It was very solid. I shook my head; I kept shaking my head. This was impossible. A mistake. But I knew it wasn't. I went to the window and looked out. My room was three storeys up.

Darkness. The surf on the beach made a white line in the moonlight.

In George's study Ysobel lay on the chaise longue, drink in hand, bottle on the table beside her. Sunlight streamed through the window. George was poring over the stock of his shotgun: it was dented, the edges splintered, and smeared with dark stains. The barrel lay on the table with the tape recorder and microphones. The Roman coins the pilot had found were in a shoe box. George ran a finger over the gun's stock, saying: "I've ruined it. Ruined it." He picked up the barrel and looked down it. "Buckled. Bent. The bloody thing'd explode if I fired it."

"You don't need to fire it," said Ysobel.

"Don't I? Don't I? What if she escapes. What if she *tries* to escape?"

"Where to? We're on an island. Anyway, she'll soon be settled. Reconciled. She knows she belongs here. Your gun is no earthly help."

"And the planes? Who's going to scare off the planes?"

"We could do without visits from the military police."

Conniach steered his boat towards the island's harbour. He was bringing two sheep and several large boxes. Ysobel sat in the boat's centre seat, wrapped in her shawl. As they came into the bay, Conniach cut the outboard engine and reached for an oar. He poled the boat to the jetty. Conniach jumped out, and Ysobel threw him the mooring rope. Taking Conniach's hand, Ysobel pulled herself out. Conniach got back in and passed out the boxes.

George appeared on the jetty. His face was grimy and dark with stubble, his clothes torn, his hands caked with earth. He was carrying a tray with a bottle, glasses and a tin of biscuits. "Provisions!" he called, set down the tray and poured three drinks. He handed one to Ysobel, who stood by the boxes, and another to Conniach, who was still in the boat. They raised their glasses in a toast. "To the rams," said George. "They're ewes," said Conniach. "To the ewes, then!"

They drank. George handed out biscuits. "We're very sorry," he said.

"Sorry?" said Conniach.

"About Uistean."

"Ah yes. Yes. A good boy, to us, he was." He looked up at George, and sniffed.

"Yes," he said. "We're sorry."

I stood at the window of my room. I saw Conniach. I heard him. I opened the window and leant out. And shouted: "Conniach! Conniach!! Connia . . . a . . . a . . . ch!!!"

Conniach chewed a biscuit. At the same time he was untying the rope that attached his boat to the jetty.

I screamed: "Help me! Conniach, please help me." But the house was far from the shore; my voice blew in the wind.

Conniach cast off the boat, pushed away from the jetty with the oar and lowered the outboard into the water.

I clutched at the window frame, leaning way out. "Conniach!! Conn . . . i . . . i . . . a . . . ach!!!" The name in the wind.

Conniach started the outboard, faced the boat towards the mainland, waved to Ysobel and George, gunned the motor. The boat's bow lifted, the stern down, the outboard churning a wake.

I knelt at the window. My cheeks were wet with tears. "Conniach. Conniach."

Conniach's boat disappeared round the headland. The sea was flat, blue, sparkling. Gulls floated against the sky. Terns splashed into the shallows.

George stood at the door to my room. He was carrying a tray with a dish, two plates, slices of homemade bread, two glasses of wine and a jug of water. He put the tray on the floor, reached into his pocket, pulled out a large key and unlocked the door. He slowly pushed it inward and peered round into the room.

I was sitting below the window, wrapped in a blanket. On the floor near me was a chamber pot half full of urine. The room was strewn with books pulled from shelves and clothes taken from a chest of drawers. Old books and old clothes, dusty and tattered. The bed was unmade, the sheets half pulled onto the floor, the blankets in a tangled heap. The bedside light was on.

George came in, opened the door wide enough to be able to reach in the tray, which he set down on the bed. He closed the door, locked it behind him and came over to me. He picked up the pot and moved it to the door. He took the tray off the bed and brought it to me. He reached out and shook my shoulder, waking me. Though I was not asleep.

I looked up and saw George's stubbled, dirty face beside mine; his blackened hands and torn fingernails resting still on my shoulder.

"Dinner," said George. "Borscht."

I looked at the tray. Then at the closed door with my pot in front of it. I stood up.

"We could eat at the table, or on the bed," said George.

"Yes," I said.

George picked up the tray and carried it to the bed. He spooned borscht onto the plates. I went over to sit beside him. George ate. I picked up a piece of bread and dipped it in the borscht.

"I've found a piece of a jug," said George. "Celtic but Roman design. And more coins. Drink?"

He passed me a glass. I shook my head. George said: "You must eat and drink. You must be strong."

"Why?"

"Why? To get well again."

"I'm not ill."

"I think you are."

"With what? Imprisonment?"

"With the mind. The imagination. False beliefs."

"In what?"

"Separation. Fragmentation. Barbarism."

"You're mad," I said. "You're mad."

"Mad? I suppose I am. We all are. But we can rejoin, you know."

"I want to leave, to go home."

"Home? What is that? I mean, where?"

"Where I live."

"But you live alone." George's voice was very quiet. "Separate. That can not be a home. Split from yourself."

"I live with friends." I knew I sounded shrill. I tried not to be. "In a house." I did not have clear feelings. More a weariness, a longing to hear other voices.

"No, no. Not *friends*. Not in a *house*. Here is a chance to be whole. The rational principle: unity, wholeness."

"You *are* mad." But I could hear the tiredness in my words. I stood up and walked over to the door. I tried the handle, pulled against the lock. I turned to face George, saying:

"Will you let me out? Now. Please."

"Yes," said George. "If that's what you *really* want." Again he came over to me. "Yes." He held his arms out to me. "Come, we are all murderers. None of us can leave. A prison of misfortune. But we can make a completeness of it. If we are rational. Sensible. Come. I'm a man." He touched my shoulders, caressed me. I closed my eyes. I began to cry.

"No, leave me alone. Please." My words stumbled through my sobs.

"I can't leave you alone. None of us can. You are us. We are you, you see. Don't you understand? We *need* you. We *are* you." And George leaned himself against me. He said: "Your softness warms me." He closed his eyes and sighed to himself.

I searched my room for something to write with. Under a cushion of an old armchair I found a stub of pencil. I tore a blank end page from a book. I wrote a message, to the world, to say where I was imprisoned. I folded the paper and attached it to a length of wool. I took this to the window and let it blow away in the wind. I watched the message with its tail of wool float off, dip, rise, then flutter down towards the sea.

In the water, the soggy piece of paper and its wool string lifted and fell with the waves. Almost submerged. A tiny speck of nothing. Invisible. Sunk.

Ysobel sat in the armchair in my bedroom. Crumbs, dirty plates, dead flowers in a vase. I was in bed, half lying and part covered by a blanket. I said: "I don't understand. Why are you keeping me here?"

"Keeping you here?" Ysobel managed a tone of real surprise. "*You* came to *us*."

"I'm a prisoner here!"

"A prisoner?" Still there was surprise in Ysobel's voice.

"Yes," I said. "I want to get off this island. I need to get home."

There was a long silence. Ysobel got up and looked out of the window. She saw George on the ground near the wall of the house. He was digging a new trench. She said, to me: "You're changing. Settling. I can feel it. As if it were in my own soul."

"Why is this door locked? Why must I piss and shit in a pot?"

"Does George lock the door? I suppose he is frightened you'll break."

"Break? Or break out? I just don't understand what's happening."

Ysobel moved over to me, sat on the bed, and reached out to me. She caught hold of my arms. Her fingers seemed to be pressing into my bones. "We lost you," she said. "You went away from us. Can't you understand that? I was alone here. In myself. Without *you* there is no youth, no fullness, no real hope. Now we must get you back. Reabsorb you. Don't you see? Won't you help? You don't want me to die, old and ugly, on this island. *I'm* the prisoner."

"And George?" I felt sudden anger, almost as a relief.

"And George," said Ysobel. "He is part of me. An insufficient part. A fraction. But with you as well, the three of us can be whole. You bring the life."

Again, silence. Ysobel got up from the bed, slowly letting her arms fall from mine, saying: "Think about it. Stay here. Give us a chance, won't you?" She walked to the door, opened it, went out, and shut it gently behind her. As if trying not to wake a sleeping child.

I looked at the door for a moment, then went over to it. I took hold of the handle, turned, and pulled. The door was not locked. I looked out into the gloomy hallway. I closed the door again. Quietly. Firmly. I let go of the handle and went back to the bed. I climbed on and curled up, hugging my knees. My anger had passed, and with it my sense of relief. Everything seemed strangely simple. I was tired.

Ysobel stood by the old portable record player in George's study. George, tape recorder hanging from his shoulder and the earphones around his neck, was drawing the cork from a bottle of wine. An empty bottle and two glasses stood on the table — with the shotgun and an array of recording equipment. Ysobel put on the Connie Francis record: "Stupid Cupid you're a real mean guy." George poured two glasses. They toasted each other and drank.

George chanted: "Yes . . . Yes . . . obel. Will you, would you, won't you care to dance?" Ysobel chanted back: "Will I, won't I, might I, shan't I, surely I shall dance."

Still holding their glasses, they took hold of each other and began to sway together cheek to cheek. George tried to waltz. But Ysobel began to follow the Connie Francis rhythm. George insisted on his waltz time. Ysobel tripped. George, clutching at her, clinging to her, almost fell to the floor.

"If you'll excuse me," said Ysobel, "I'll change the . . . Conductor! A waltz if you please!"

With a bow she disengaged from George, went to the record player, and jerked the needle off the record. George steadied himself against the table. Then he put on his headphones and connected a microphone to his tape recorder. Ysobel held out her arms, ready to resume the waltz. George, humming a waltz tune, held the microphone in one hand, Ysobel in the other. They attempted a few steps. "Wait, bum tum. Here, tum dee. Listen, tum dah."

George took off the headphones and put them on Ysobel's head. She was wired to the tape recorder. George hummed. They danced. Through the headphones Ysobel could hear amplified humming and scuffles and bangs.

"Here. Wait," said George. "Listen to this." George took the microphone and pressed it against Ysobel's heart, stomach, chest. The thumps and gurgles of her insides boomed into her ears. Then she heard a new sound, of footsteps. Ysobel looked puzzled. Where were these other sounds coming from? She looked around her and saw me, in jeans and T-shirt, barefoot, hollow eyed, standing in the doorway. Ysobel froze. George, intent on recording more of Ysobel's body sounds, had not noticed me. Ysobel pulled off the earphones. I stepped into the room.

"Come," said Ysobel. "Come and dance."

"Yes." George had turned and seen me. "Dance with us." Both of them held out hands to me. I moved towards them, and took their hands.

We danced together. Ysobel and I waltzed; George, with his arms round the two of us, danced sideways, like an agitated crab, humming in waltz time. The record had stopped. Ysobel murmured soothingly into my ear. My eyes were shut tight.

The three of us bumped into the chaise longue. Ysobel lurched backwards and sat down on its seat. George fell sideways, tumbling against Ysobel. I was left standing.

I opened my eyes, took a step backwards, causing Ysobel's hand to lose its hold on my arm. Ysobel and George clutched at one another, shaking with laughter. I turned and walked to the door.

I walked over the grassy headland between the white house and the beach. It was a midsummer night. The sun was setting on the sea.

Ysobel came out of the front door of the white house. She stopped. George appeared beside her. The headphones trailing behind him. He was carrying his shotgun. They both squinted into the night and struggled to keep their balance.

I walked along the beach, towards the sea.

Ysobel ran towards the shore. "Marianne! No! Don't! No!" She tried to run faster, but tripped and fell to her knees. She tried to get up, but she was old, suddenly, and frail. Her hair thin and grey. Her cheeks sunken, without make-up. Her lips without rouge. She crawled towards the sea, calling: "Marianne! No!"

I waded out into the sea. I was up to my waist. I kept wading.

George walked towards the beach. Hurrying. Microphone and earphones trailing behind him. He passed the pale, weak Ysobel on her knees. He opened the shotgun and loaded cartridges into both barrels. Ysobel shouted to him. "Stop her! For God's sake stop her!"

I swam away from the beach.

George raised the shotgun to his shoulder, aimed, and fired. The barrel burst. The shattered gun dropped from George's hands. For a moment he was still, as if the smoke that obscured his face held him. Then he fell, clutching his eyes. Blood was seeping between his fingers.

I swam. But I was tiring. I gasped for breath and forced myself on. The light was fading, the sun disappearing into the horizon. The waves were terribly dark.

I trod water, panting, shivering. I swam for a while on my back. I stopped, trod water again. Then I rolled up onto my side, and swam on. I was cold. But had no fear. I had few thoughts, little more than a will to live. I was just able to keep going. The light was gone. I was so cold. The sea broke on the rocks of an invisible shoreline.

In the darkness of the night and the waves, I realized that I was no longer able to swim. Barely able to move at all. My mouth was filling with water. I flailed, raising myself for a moment into air. I breathed. And dropped back again, sinking. Breathing in water. I was drowning.

The sea broke on black rocks, on dark sands: a pale line of foam and surf was all that revealed a shore.

Light. Greenish light. As if the other side of the sea. Or a glimmer of patterns through opaque glass. Shapes. Shadows or movements on the light. A murmur of voices.

The shapes become more distinct. The shadow of a head. The vague features of a face. The voice of a man. A Scottish accent. "She's moving. Her eyes. Marianne!"

I can see a dome of apparatus: drip feeds, oxygen mask, monitors. The array of equipment above and around a patient in intensive care. I can not understand. A woman's voice is speaking to me with strange urgency. "Can you see me? Open your eyes wider. Try and look at me." I hear myself groan. The sound is so close to me — like the sounds through headphones. I begin to mutter: "where . . . where . . . ?" I squint; the dome, the apparatus becomes less clear.

The woman's voice again, so close to me: "You're in hospital. Don't worry. You'll be alright. You had a crash. Breathe easy now. Try and keep your eyes open. Breathe now. Good!"

But I can not hold my eyes open. I want to say: don't worry, I've escaped, there is no danger. Only the rest of time. My mouth won't form the words. Somewhere, in the distance, the Scottish voice again. "Marianne, say something. Can you hear us? Say something to us." I want to say: the light is green, at the other side of the sea. I hear my voice, so close again. I say to them, whoever they are up there: "Where have I been?"

I look at myself in the mirror. One side of my face is marked by the large scab of a newly healed cut. How long has this been healing? They told me I could leave. That it was safe for me to drive. That the car was at a garage. They have brought it for me, here. Everything arranged. One wing of the car is part buckled, part missing. A wheel wobbles. The windscreen has a web of cracks across one side. But it goes.

A nurse says to me: "Where were you going?"
"On holiday. To the island."
A look of worry in her eyes. "Will there be anyone else there?"
"Yes," I say. "My boyfriend."

I leave the hospital. I put on a head scarf and leave. I turn onto a main road and towards the shores of the lough. I dive along a steep headland, following a narrow road cut into the rocks. Below the road, below the car, the sea rolls against the shore. I pull up at the end of a dirt track across a field. The track leads to a beach, where we played in our summer holidays. This was our farthest horizon. I seem never to have seen it before. I get out, lean against the car, and look out to sea.

The island. The large white house. Apart from a few sheep, everything is deserted. I know that this is how it always was. I must find the key, get the boat out. How hard to remember things: my mind stands in the present. But under the stones, yes, under the stones. There *is* a key, and the door does open, like it used to. And there *is* a boat, the way there always was. I can free the door, get in, and drag the boat out — it is fibreglass with the lightest of oars. Everything, now, is automatic. The boat the oars the slide down the beach to the water's edge.

I go back to the car and fetch a bag, lock the car doors, and go back to the dinghy. I throw the bag into it, and wade into the water. Cold water and seething shingle: my feet are alive! I face the dinghy into the waves, clamber in, and row towards the island. Round the headland that shelters the bay and its jetty below the white house. Past flotillas of weed, a line of rocks that narrow the harbour entrance. Until the dinghy is grounded on the sand. I jump out, grab the dinghy, and pull it up beyond the sea's reach. My skin is alive with the happiness of so many simple movements.

And there, close by, stands the white house. I swing my bag onto my shoulder, feeling strong. I head up to the doorway of the house, pull it open and look inside the hallway. My body is like air, without thoughts.

Along the corridor, into the kitchen. Deserted. A pair of muddy boots on the floor; curtains flap at part-open windows; the messy remains of a meal on the kitchen table; the fire door of the range open, with a spill of ash on the floor. I am not sure which way to go. I hesitate, then decide: I pick up the boots lying on the kitchen floor and take down an old coat from a peg behind the door.

In coat and boots, I am walking across the island. The grass is like a thin sponge under my feet. The wind pulls at me. I am at the height of the land: beyond stretches the sea, broken by the black outline of rocks and islets: horizon and sky. Beyond the shore far below me, among weeds and thin reefs far away, I can see a boat. Tiny, rising and falling, above and below the edges of the waves. My throat catches with unexpected excitement. I stop and stare. Into the wind that makes my eyes water. I realize there is a taste of salt on my lips. The boat turns, and moves further out. I recognize the boat!

I begin to run, plunging down the slopes of the island's land, running in line with the sea. I stumble, fall, pick myself up, run on.

I arrive at the beach, panting, dishevelled. I wave and scream: "Ahoy! Hey! Ahoy!" A figure in the boat is hauling on a rope that leads down into the sea. The engine of his outboard is idling; the wind is offshore; he doesn't hear my yells. "Hey!!! Uistean!!!"

In his boat, Uistean is hauling a lobster pot out of the water. The pot breaks the surface: there is a lobster in it. He tugs the pot over the gunwale and begins to untie the thong holding the wicker trap shut. Other pots are stacked in the boat's bow. He hears something. He raises his head from the pot and looks towards the shore. He sees me. I am standing on the shore waving both my arms, laughing with relief. Uistean throws out the line and lobster pot, freeing the boat, grabs the oars and rows towards me.

Uistean's boat nudges inside the weed and reefs that line the shore beyond me. I wade to my knees and clutch the boat's gunwale. Uistean reaches out and catches my arm. I lean towards him. We try and kiss. But the boat moves; I put my arms around him to steady her. We are both laughing. I give myself a pull against the boat and the man, and swing aboard. The boat almost capsizes. Uistean throws himself to the other side of the boat to offset my weight. The boat rocks. I tumble in, thumping against the lobster pots. Laughing, laughing. Alive. In the present.

We — Uistean and I — are in the kitchen of the white house. Uistean is crouched beside the range, trying to get damp wood to blaze. I am sitting at the table eating a sandwich. I am still wearing my head scarf.

"I thought no one was here."

"You saw the stuff on the table. The mess!"

"Seemed old. Stale."

"A man on his own, eh?"

"I suppose."

Uistean closes the fire door of the range, stands, reaches up to a cupboard and pulls down a can of beer and a tin of sardines. He sits at the table and opens them, tipping the sardines onto a plate already dotted with grease and bread crumbs. He takes a swig from the beer and passes it to me. I take a swig. It makes me shudder; I pass it back to Uistean.

"Revolting. On top of the stuff they gave me at the hospital."

"Did you do yourself much damage?

"Cuts and bruises. Concussion. Nothing broken. Just brain damage." He looks so serious; I laugh. "When you're drunk enough I'll give you a surprise."

"Do I have to wait that long?"

"You used to be able to get there soon enough!"

"That was *last* summer."

"Yes. Yes it was."

There is silence between us. Then I say, "Uistean, I'm going to do it." Uistean avoids my eyes. "I've got the stuff."

"It was in the car!! Marianne!"

"No timer, no bang."

"Marianne, let's talk about it later."

"There's no one else on the island is there?"

"Let's talk about it later."

The study. Night. The table is clear but covered with a film of dust. The gun cupboard stands closed. The bookshelves have a scatter of popular paperbacks — Agatha Christie, Dick Francis. Tidy, dusty, unused. It all seems so long ago and yet so close.

I am sitting on the chaise longue. Uistean is kneeling in front of me, his head resting face down on my lap. Buried in my skirt. I want to stroke his hair. For once — or at last — the anger has gone. I think: have I now made so much peace with myself that I can let him in to me?

"Uistean, does this place never give you the creeps?" He is so vulnerable, so much alone. Are we two children in a private compartment of our own? His boat. The empty house. Two wounded children. But my anger is gone. Drowned perhaps. The thought makes me smile. Then shudder. "I always used to love it. Childhood summers. The family outpost. A place where even *my* mother managed a kind of inner peace." I realize that I am musing aloud. "The yearly pilgrimage. Splashing about. On the surface, I suppose. Huh!" I look down at Uistean. He is burrowing his head into my lap. He has a hand on one of my knees. It feels warm and strong. As if it can keep those strange bones in place. "I always felt free here. Especially with you. Did you feel the same? The sea opened me up. Hey, you're laughing down there. Are you ready for your surprise?"

I catch hold of Uistean's hair and tilt his head back so I can look right at him. But his eyes are closed. "Open your eyes." With my other hand I reach up to my head scarf and pull it off. I am completely bald.

"Jesus Christ!"

"Like it?"

Uistean stares.

"Feel it. Go on." I take hold of his hand and lay it in on my head. "Do you think I need a shave?"

"I expected something worse."

"Semtex? It's in my bag. Sounds like the newest kind of sanitary towel."

Silence.

"Listen, Uistean. You don't have to do anything."

"It was my idea."

"So you've changed your mind. Now it's my idea. I got the stuff. I want to do it. I really want to do it. All you have to do is give me a ride. You're the boatman. Innocent guide. The caretaker I asked to take me on an outing. We'll be fishing. I'll have a picnic bag. You'll say you knew nothing." Silence. "That's the way I want it."

"And getting back?"

"Not your problem."

"Marianne, I want you to give it up."

"I know. But I haven't any choice. I realized in the hospital. If anyone ever asks you what it takes, tell them: a bang on the head."

"But why?"

"Hatred. I'm so full of hatred. About the world. I can't live with this anger. And it's not a *disease*. Not some kind of madness. Do you know what I'm talking about?" I look at him. "I don't want paralysis. I don't want to be helpless. Up here you might not feel it. But you *must* feel it." I pause, I need to think. "The power of evil. That's what the planes are. I have to do something to get it out. Out of me. And out of the world. At least a bit of it. One bit. Out."

I think: I haven't said it right. I haven't explained the anger. I haven't talked about Didi and George and the hopelessness, of how they gripped . . . I feel the tears coming. I am determined to be calm. I have escaped. I tell myself, I have escaped. At last. I can act, now. Not in freedom, but in my own right. Does that mean nothing? I must breathe deeply; I must let myself sit back in the chaise longue.

"You'll take me, Uistean. On a picnic. Up the shore. You have to."

His eyes are so unclear. He looks up at me with an emptiness on his face. Can he understand so little? He says: "I want you. I'm a man. I want to lie against you."

I say: "Like last summer? Like before?"

"No, no. It is different now. I mean, you are different."

"Bald? A scar on my head!"

"Damn it, Marianne. You are a woman. More than ever. Like never before."

"Yes, I think I am. At last. But not for you."

"Is there someone else?"

I don't know what to say. Silence so often means yes.

"Then I'll borrow you."

How ridiculous he seems. I think (terrible thought!): poor boy, stuck on his island, Conniach's heir, owner of a hillside by a lough.

"You'll take me, Uistean. On a picnic."

Uistean is steering his fishing boat along the mainland coast. Lobster pots piled in the bow. Me sitting in the centre, beside a large picnic basket and a half-empty, recorked bottle of wine. I am holding a fishing rod. The sun is low in the sky; it is not long after dawn.

The boat moves down a narrow lough.

A wire fence runs along the lough's shore. Beyond the fence Uistean's boat has stopped. Uistean is setting a lobster pot. I am fishing. From here I can see the wire fence and a guard post. A sentry is sitting beside a gate in the wire fence.

Uistean's boat is at the mouth of a sandy bay. Uistean is letting another pot down into the sea. There are only two left in the boat. I am holding the basket in my lap. Time is like the air, flowing around me, holding me in one place, outside of me. I feel free.

"Take me ashore. Leave me here."

"Marianne . . . "

"Here, Uistean. This is where the old path goes. Where we played as children."

"It won't be the same."

"It is. I checked."

Uistean turns the boat into the bay, nudging slowly into the shallows. I wave my right arm.

"A bit more this way. The mussel rock, remember."

Uistean turns the boat.

"Straight now."

The boat straightens and runs aground. I jump out, carefully taking my picnic basket with me.

Beside the gate in the fence, the sentry is dozing.

I push Uistean's boat off the sand. Uistean poles through the shadows.

"See to your pots, Uistean. Fish. Make your way back to the island. Be natural."

"I could come and meet you."

"No. Go back. I'll go to my car. You won't see me."

"I'll meet you at the car."

"You won't. You *must* go back to the island. Promise me."

The boat is well clear of the sand. Uistean is trailing the oar in the sea. I am holding the gunwale: facing it into the waves, supporting my weight.

"Promise me, Uistean."

"I promise."

Uistean lowers the oar into the boat and sits down. He is staring at me.

"Hey, I forgot the wine!" I catch hold of the boat with one hand and reach out with the other. Uistean picks up the wine and hands it to me. I take it and let go of the boat.

"Take care, caretaker."

I turn and wade back towards the shore.

Uistean, face wrinkled with misery, rows the boat out of the bay. Hesitating between strokes, using enough strength to keep the boat moving forwards.

I walk through the long grass that grows on the shoreline dune. A steep slope, and the grass catching at my legs. I should have worn jeans. I laugh at myself: for this, a skirt is the right costume. I make my way across and up. Being circumspect. The grass-covered bank shivers in the breeze, its ridge far above me.

I reach the top of the dunes. I am puffing with the effort. I must sit on the ground. I put down the picnic basket beside me. I want to drink, I want to feel wine in my throat, I want to toast Uistean in the distance. I raise the wine bottle to my mouth, its cork in my teeth, and pull. I spit the cork into the grass and drink. I put the bottle down. I sit for a moment, listening.

Out to sea: nothing, no boats, not even Uistean's. Along the shore: grassy dunes, beach, no one. Above me: the top of the ridge, the sky.

I take hold of the picnic basket, lower myself into the grass, and crawl to the ridge, keeping my head below its peak. I lie down and squirm, on my belly. Slowly, slowly. I must keep myself hidden in the grass, but I raise my head high enough to see over the ridge.

I see the wire fence, and through it two lines of low-flying bombers. A black and perfect symmetry. Beyond the planes is the concrete flight control and security tower. I must crawl a bit farther; I must look along the fence, towards the gate where the guard is dozing. I begin crawling forwards, down the other side of the ridge, towards the fence.

The guard by the gate opens his eyes, looks at his watch, rearranges himself in his chair, and closes his eyes.

I am at the fence. I open the picnic basket. I need the wire cutters. I lift them, oh I lift them with such care, from among small, fat envelopes and tiny digital clocks. I close the basket. I begin to cut the fence. Uistean comes into my mind. I imagine him as he steers his boat through rocks. Now the bow will be empty, and ride high in the sea. I expect he is going fast, purposefully. The cutters clip the fence with surprising ease.

The air is so still. I can hear the sounds of the sentry post. Footsteps. A phone rings. I freeze and listen to a voice, the sentry's voice. "Jameson here. Roger. Roger. A-OK." I breathe again.

I squat beside the hole in the fence. The wire cutters are lying in the grass; I won't need them any more. I must set the clocks, and attach each one.

Suddenly I see the sentry. He is walking some fifteen yards away, looking out to sea. He is watching the sun, the sea, the horizon. I wonder if he can see Uistean. I wonder if he is watching Uistean looking towards us, trying to get a view towards the mainland, carrying the fishing rod.

I breathe. I stand up, basket in hand, and walk across the grass that separates the wire fence from the runway. Without haste. Without looking around. I have almost reached the nearest plane. I open the basket. Now. Now I must run.

At the sentry post the panel of lights begins flashing and the phone rings. The sound of an alarm buzzer. Running. Everyone seems to be running. I have escaped. First one, then another. One packet here, one packet over there. Running. I must keep running. Zigzag escape. From plane to plane. The smoke is filling my lungs, covering me, hiding me. And the noise, the bells and the sirens. I must run to the left, towards the fence. But I can't move. I must cover my head. Here is another blast. I must breathe out, breathe out, keep out the smoke. I realize I am waiting for pain. I must breathe. For the freedom of this moment will be short. I must reach and escape them all. I think: "Everything has disappeared."

Uistean is standing on a rock on the height of the ridge beside the island's jetty. The fishing rod is on the grass beside him. He is staring at the curve of the land in the distance. A flash of red flame bursts out of the far shoreline. A moment of silence. Uistean steps forwards, as if there were a bridge between him and the flames. Then the boom of an explosion. Another flash. Another boom. A pall of smoke. Another flash, more smoke, the red of a huge fire. More blasts. More smoke.

The surf rolls on the sea's edge. Sea birds call. Tide pools, flotillas of seaweed, rocks, a beach, the marks of a boat's hull in the sand, and footprints. There are footprints up the beach, to shingle, to grasses, to a shack with its door hanging open, to a battered VW beetle, one wing smashed in, one wheel awry, parked there, small against the wide shore. The little road is a thread at the base of the cliff, leading from the dotlike car to a vast and empty land.

THE
LAKE

Sara died. Not long ago. In Brighton. A dull little town, for all its notoriety. A fish-and-chip shop steak-and-kidney pie place, despite the pier, which is gone now anyway. She died in England.

This is my wife's story. Sara *was* my wife. Sometimes I have thought: without my knowing it, in an absence of mind, we have twisted our way in and out of God damned history. In and out of Europe. Death in the wings, those on stage "alive enough to have strength to die." Thomas Hardy's line. Though he was speaking of love, not history. And he lived in England. Hardy, that is. She lived on the shadow. Thin, like a stick.

Age is the shadow, now.

She was twenty-six. Sara. Abraham's wife. Anyone who converts to Judaism receives the Hebrew name Avram ben Avram, son of Abraham. What do they call the women? Sara bat Avram. But that would be the wife of the husband. Theology wearies me. She was a Jewess. I did not even think of conversion. She was the traveller — not a gipsy, but like a gipsy with her dark eyes and no possessions and her music.

My eyes were green when we met. Now they are grey, and watery, and look backwards. I am wrinkled, the whole in the style of the testicles. Love was a bond between us always.

We met in Brighton. She was a DP, displaced person. She had no one. A job in a bed and breakfast place that belonged to my mother's best friend. Who wanted to do something about "all those poor people, adrift." She enjoyed the word. "Adrift. In a sea of change, the creature." My mother's friend had grown up in Dublin.

"The creature" brought us coffee on an imitation silver tray. My mother and I had come for a morning visit. "This is Sara," said my mother's friend. "I told you about her, didn't I? Her English is excellent, already." She led Sara into displaying her English. And her eyes that seemed to jump from side to side. Her pale skin. Her fingers, so delicately shaped. Her black hair. The frailty of being so alone, so foreign; yet she exuded strength. As I looked at her I could feel her — in my memory I seem to feel her — flowing into my being, filling me out, making me complete. And I wanted, immediately, to take care of her.

I took her to the pictures. On the pier. To dances — she was a wonderful dancer. We took care of each other.

I was ten years older than her, but even as she danced, even when she laughed, even as a person whom I felt I must protect, she seemed to have a wisdom far beyond mine. A poise. A strength to be any age. As if she belonged in the fabric of the world on which I had now arrived. She had such youth, but when I heard her voice, or touched her, I somehow felt I was a newcomer. I think back to that time, our first times together. When she was, I thought, my Sara.

So much ought to lie between then and now. Apart from the story, there is so little. My mind drifts.

She became a Catholic. Why a Catholic? I said, be a real Christian, be English. I offered her the English Church. Automatic membership. But no, nothing automatic for Sara. She had to go through the business of joining. Some need for belonging and hence, perhaps, for exclusion. Or a need for mother right: a faith for which maternity defines the children's membership. Or perhaps she understood, as I never did, that our affair required a more than secular divide — a gulf across which we reached, without which we would not touch. Love of the body requires difference. We who are old know this too well: in our drooped encasements each becomes like the other: achievement of life's most unwelcome unity.

I listened to her stories. She said I didn't. I asked her to tell me what had happened. She said I showed no interest.

There were too many stories. Hers, and then everyone else's. She often paused when telling about some part of her journeys and travails (no other, less old-fashioned word does justice to the mixture of work and suffering, work and suffering that became the one and only way of life for her). She paused, and interrupted herself, saying of whoever had now appeared in the narrative — "Ah, *she* had a story." Always glimpsed, touched, untold. Stories crisscrossing one another, holding one another in place, like the tendrils of a climbing plant, sparse and yet with deceptive strength. Each story bending to help the other. Each one a story in itself, but seen to be impossible of comprehension without another. The incidents arriving, again and again, at a point beyond which they could not go without the sequence of someone else's incidents. Webs of stories, spun spiderwise backwards and forwards, round and round; stories that would be complete as a spider's web if only all the parts could be told.

At first she had no great need to tell. More likely, she had a need to be silent. To be accepted. To feel my hands gentle on her back, our arms touching silently. To be away from it all. We found each other in the silences, though never, I believe, without some knowledge — a peaceful silence, this — of what had happened. Or so I thought. In the aftermath, how does one speak with the dispossessed if not with broad hands and few words? The unspeakable must remain what it is. I felt her grief; touched it; in my way, contained it. That much I did know, but was wrong to have believed that I knew much more. I never asked myself what it was I did not know. I did not think: this person, this partner, eludes me. I did not search for the underlying truths, the absences. What does one do with the possibility of discovering a void? I did not examine our daily lives. I lived them, more or less happily. I thought. Or, day by day, I did not *think*. Brighton was so far away from all that.

She cried in the night. I did not ask, "What are you crying about?" I suppose that her answers — the only possible answers — would have had no meaning: history, fate. Or: the war, what the Germans did. Or: the impossibility of words. I held her when her weeping woke me. Often, no doubt, I snored through it all.

She was not possessed by demons, not tyrannized by unnamed terrors. Grief from the depths is not like fear or anger or neurosis. Grief is the mist that hides stories that are not yet ready to be told. The outlines of these stories are thin, their substances much less than that which surrounds them. Fragments of such stories can not explain the feelings, and the sum of them — their collectivity — is inchoate. Or the grief could have been the frame on which the tendrils of her stories might have seized and climbed. She might, in the early days, allude to a story or refer to some episode in her former life. But she did not expect me, then — I don't believe she then expected me — to ask for the story, for the elaboration of the details. I met her, rather, in the mist; and felt the grief which, from time to time, swelled within her and spilled over.

Like the bursting of a boil, and the pus a relief from the core's infection. Should I have lanced the thing, released to the core, allowed the pus in torrents? Is my failure to ask for the stories this failure of the lance? She was ready to tell me, much later.

She was old, already, when she began.

If she had had children — I mean, if we had had a child — she might have spoken sooner. She might have wanted the child to know. She might have held out a hand and said, come with me to your grandparents' home, to the places you would visit if they had survived. Though I wonder how you lead a child by the hand to the deformities of the world, without deforming it. And I wonder how you share with a child the very forces — grief, despair, brutality — from which every parental instinct surely causes you to wish that the child be protected. Might Sara have preferred to avoid this parental dilemma by choosing not to be a parent?

She wanted children, she said, and sometimes mourned our infertility. She blamed it on "things that had happened." Should I have said, "What things? Of the body or the inner self?" I could not ask, with any ease, with any pleasure in discovering more about this person I loved — to ask was to feel dread, of what happened, of what was done to others, or what might have been done to her. We shared childlessness, but I knew that the damage had been done to her body, not mine. She was alive. A price of survival might have been to live without stories.

1946-89: a time of no stories. Then they pulled the wall down. I said to Sara: "We must go to Berlin." She said nothing for a while. A day. Two days. Then: "I think we should. But how?" "We'll drive." "Yes," she said. "We'll drive."

On the way she told me the basic story. She told it to me, in the car, as we drove in the slow lanes of the motorways and autobahns, a hesitant old couple. Though, as she talked, as she took me closer to her than I had been in years, I felt young, the age when we met: hearing Sara's memory as if she recalled every sound, every word: such detail that she took me across the years, to a time when, for both of us, the world lay ahead. Two old duffers with eyes sparkling! No, I was old, she still ageless. And the new landscapes outside.

I did not ask Sara to fill in the gaps. She started as if at the next episode of a series, or saga, that was already under way. She had forgotten that this was a beginning. Of course, she might have chosen to leave the actual beginning in perpetual hiding. Escape was the point. She needed to explain that she had survived, without shame, free of guilt. And she left every detail of survival vivid in my mind.

I've taken what she said. And made her story, a part of her story, the piece she led me into. With few supporting tendrils; or a web's centre, hopelessly incomplete. I have made this story, her story, close to her words, as a memorial. I imagine, if she and I together had led a quite different life, there might have been a memorial gathering. If we had had a community of friends, these friends might have met one afternoon, and shared a memory of Sara. If she had not been hidden, had not been so alone; if we had not bound one another together; if I had been less English, less uneasy about my wife's difference, her strangeness and estrangement; if the world had shaped otherwise, then, at the memorial gathering I would have read out these words:

Somewhere in central Asia they came to a lake so wide that even on the clearest day no one could see one side from the other.

The three women climbed down into the divide between forest and lake. Between the dark pines of the forest and lake's cold water, driftwood trunks and branches evoked every part of the human body.

The women found themselves in a surreal maze which, as it followed the circle of the shoreline, was infinite.

"We must build a raft," said Sara.

Rebecca answered her: "With no axe and no rope, you imagine a raft!"

Katerina looked at the water of the lake. She walked to its edge, bent and untied her laces, pulled off the boots, hoisted her trousers to her knees and waded calf-deep. "Cold," she said. "But good. Let's swim."

"You're crazy," shouted Rebecca.

But Sara had already sat on a driftwood branch and was pulling at her boots. She reached into each foot, to take out the straw she had packed on the soles to shield her feet from the cold and nails that stuck through the worn leather. She set the boots down on top of the straw: there was enough breeze to scatter it away. Dry straw was precious. Then she undressed. Army fatigues patched in a dozen places, the remains of an overcoat, a belt made of canvas strips, socks shaped out of grain sacks: these, her clothes, she put beside her boots. She stood among the dead trees, naked.

Rebecca was watching her. "Sara," she called. "You are thin like a stick." And Rebecca held up a long bony finger. "Skinny like this."

Sara looked down her body, ran her eyes over the starved bones that stretched her pale skin. She was small, but the creases of her skin showed that once she had been plump. She was eighteen, much the youngest of the three of them, yet her flesh was withered as if by age. "Yes," she said. "And filthy."

Katerina, already undressed, was wading out into the water. She was tall and broad shouldered. But under the surfaces of her skin the vertebrae stuck out like a series of clenched fists, and her shoulder blades like broken plates. When the water reached her hips, Katerina lowered her upper body into the lake, shrieked, and ducked. She came up spluttering and shouted, "It's wonderful. Freezing and wonderful!"

Sara waded out to join her. Katerina flailed her arms, spraying water all around. Sara screamed, "Stop it! I'll *freeze* to death!" But Katerina splashed her more. Water showered over Sara. Drops caught the sunlight; the air between the two women sparkled. They shouted in mock agony.

Rebecca began to take off her clothes. With a gasp at the effort of it, she raised a boot onto a log. Her fingers picked at the knots in her laces. She pushed the boot over the heel of her foot, and tugged. The sock underneath was dark with blood. She eased the boot over the foot, avoiding the wounds. She paused, and breathed, finding strength. She moved her foot, turning it to protect bloody swellings from her weight. She looked up at Katerina and Sara. They were no longer playing, but stooped side by side rubbing water into their faces. Rebecca turned and sat, sank down rather, on the log where her foot had rested. She said to the lake, to the others, to herself: "We must find food. Please God, we must find food."

Sara walked ashore, on the shingle, among the driftwood shapes. Goose pimples mottled her skin; her lips were blue, her teeth chattering with cold. She came to her clothes, gathered them up and clutched them to her. She said to Rebecca: "It's too cold." Katerina, from her pile of clothes, called out: "But it's good. Good to be clean again."

"Yes," said Sara. "A shock to the life forces. You should go in, Becki."

Katerina and Sara always called her Becki, as if to infantilize — at forty-six Rebecca was infinitely older than the others — the one on whom they so often depended. Rebecca held up the index fingers of both hands.

"Two sticks," she said. "Just like two old sticks!"

The three women followed the lakeside. They walked in single file, and here, among the driftwood forest, Rebecca chose a route that shifted from the shore to the beach head, and at times forced them to clamber over trunks and branches they could not circumnavigate. But they were weak. Rebecca knew that none of them could more than crawl over logs. Once she noticed a tree that lay parallel to the shore. She realized that they could use its long, smooth trunk as a walkway. But she also saw that the effort of climbing up its rounded sides — a mere four feet from the shingle — was too much for Sara. Rebecca helped her up, and resolved to stick to the beach.

They stopped often, and sat with eyes half closed. What did they think about? Food. Breath. Aching bones. Sore feet. Pain. Once Katerina said: "Shouldn't we try going back into the forest? It would be easier to walk. We might find a path."

"No," answered Rebecca. "We would get lost. We must stick to the lake. There's bound to be some people somewhere along the shore. Or a road."

"I don't see why," said Katerina. "Why should there be people here? There's no sign of anyone here."

Rebecca turned to look at Sara. "What do you think, Sara?"

Sara's eyes were shut. She didn't open them. She said, "I think we should do what Becki says."

Rebecca turned to Katerina. "Let's try for a day or two."

"We can't keep going *that* long," said Katerina.

"Yes we can," said Rebecca. "We'll pick berries. And there'll be some kind of village on the lake shore."

Katerina shrugged, and closed her eyes.

They followed the shore. Time was slow. The sun shone for all but two hours of midsummer twilight. They found wild strawberries and blackcurrants in patches of open ground close to the beach, in places where storms or fires had opened the forest edge and allowed grasses and shrubs to grow. They ate and, their stomachs aching, moved. On round a circumference that seemed to have so many images, but no actual footprints, of humans.

Towards the end of one such day Rebecca noticed a large break in the line of evergreens above the beach. "Look," she said. "There must be berries there. We can pick lots, perhaps. And sleep." They chose places to rest where they could find rushes or grasses to soften the ground.

They struggled over a line of driftwood that blockaded the beach between them and the clearing, then found themselves looking into much the largest opening in the forest they had seen since travelling the lakeside. Sara and Rebecca walked to the centre of the clearing and onto a wide carpet of plants from which dangled a shimmer of pink and red strawberries. They knelt and filled their hands to overflowing.

"Use your shirt," urged Rebecca. "Take off your shirt and use it as a bag. We must pick as much as we can."

"We'll be sick," said Sara. But she pulled her shirt off and arranged it into a loose pouch beside her. "The berries will stain it. I'll look good."

"These are the first really ripe berries we've found. We can risk eating more." And Rebecca pulled off her shirt too, laying it beside her among the plants.

At the far side of the clearing, among thickets of low bushes, Katerina was searching for blackcurrants. Suddenly she was shouting. "Becki, Sara! Come here! Look here!"

Sara called back. "We're in the middle of the best strawberries!"

But the urgent tone in Katerina's voice caught Rebecca's notice. She pushed herself to her feet, and tried to make out where Katerina was among the bushes. "What is it? Where are you?"

"Here. Over here!" Katerina waved. Rebecca began to walk towards her.

"What is it?"

"Someone's been cutting down trees."

When she heard this, Sara gathered her shirtful of berries into a bundle, got to her feet, and caught up to Rebecca. "It must be some kind of animal," she said. "What animals are there here?"

"I don't know," said Rebecca.

"What about people?" Sara's voice was almost a whine.

"I wonder," said Rebecca. "On the other side of the lake, perhaps. That's what Katerina heard, isn't it?"

They had said this to each other so often, had again and again shared the hope that they would find people on the other side of the lake, people who were not part of the war, people who would not want to enslave or murder them. Their steps were slow and cautious as they came towards where Katerina had stood: she had disappeared again, somewhere among the trees of the forest. They needed people, yet feared them. They walked and endured in order to reach them, on the other side of the lake. But they were escaping from people, too.

"I bet it's animals." Sara often spoke the thoughts they shared, as if she, rather than Rebecca or Katerina, had the energy to state both the obvious and the terrifying.

"Where are you? Katerina! Katerina!" Rebecca called into the trees.

"Here." The voice came from the darkness of the pines a short way to their left. "Follow the path."

A path? Rebecca and Sara both looked down and sure enough, just to the side of them was a pale line, a narrow mark where feet had worn and changed the ground.

"Animal tracks?" Sara's voice feared both that it might and might not be evidence of human beings.

They followed the pale mark and came to Katerina. She was moving her fingers over axe marks on the stump of a large birch tree. The cuts were light in colour, clean. Small chips of wood and bark were scattered around the forest floor.

"This is new isn't it? Yesterday even. Or the day before." Katerina bent and picked up some chips. "Look. Feel them. They're fresh."

"It's been very dry. They may look much newer than they are." But Rebecca rolled a chip between her fingers as if it were a bird's egg, exploring it with fearful gentleness.

"There was rain last week. It must be since then." Sara had been staring at the birch stump, and now looked off farther into the forest. Her eye caught the glimmer of more stumps. She walked a few yards. Chips and bark were scattered everywhere. Three freshly cut stumps stood in a group. "Hey! Over here! Over here."

Rebecca and Katerina joined her. They all began to explore the ground. Rebecca pointed off to one side. "Look," she said. "Someone's dragged a tree this way. Let's follow."

"Who could it be?" Sara stared at the torn ground and broken leaves and branches the dragging of the tree had caused to lie along its route. "Shouldn't we be careful?"

"Whoever it is might have food," said Katerina. "Come on. We don't have any choice."

"We have a choice," said Rebecca. "But I don't think soldiers cut down trees deep in the forest. There's all kinds of firewood right on the beach, isn't there?"

"I don't know what you mean." But Sara followed the other two anyway.

The scar on the earth led deeper into the forest. They walked in careful silence, rolling their feet to muffle their tread. Then the trail met a wider mark on the ground — almost a real path — and turned towards the lake shore. There was a gap: the trail from the forest led to an open way from the trees to the water. They stopped. The shingle of the beach was strewn everywhere with wood chips and pieces of bark. But nothing else. The three women were disappointed. Then Rebecca noticed another opening in the driftwood, leading off to the side. She walked just far enough to see that it led to a sort of entrance way among the driftwood beyond which was a wide patch of open, the shingle and sand tramped flat and smooth by many feet. She gasped.

This opening showed all the signs of a campsite. A huge pile of blackened wood ash marked a central fireplace. All around were crude shelters, or the frames for shelters, built with driftwood branches. Old skins, shaped bits of wood, circles of stones.

"There must have been a hundred people here," said Sara.

"I doubt it," said Rebecca. "A family, I think."

"But who are they? Where have they gone?" Sara's voice was again full of unease.

"Herders. They must have been building rafts or boats. To cross the lake." Rebecca spoke as she examined the ashes of the fire. "Cold. But dry. They left after it last rained. But more than a day or two ago."

"Might they be back?"

"Don't worry, Sara," said Rebecca. "If they are herders, they've gone for the rest of the summer. To join their animals across the lake, to avoid the flies."

"There aren't many flies," said Sara.

"But there will be. Where's Katerina gone?" Rebecca looked up from the ashes and peered at the driftwood lean-tos around them. "Katerina! Where are you?"

"They kill the herders too, don't they?"

"Yes," said Rebecca. "Because they're primitive. That's what they say. Being primitive is one of the things that's not allowed."

"They should see us," said Sara. "We've become primitive."

"Yes," said Rebecca. "That's just what they would say. Come on, let's look for Katerina. Where did she go?"

They found Katerina, heard her rather, in among a heap of driftwood. She called out to them: "Come in here. I've found something else."

"Where are you?" said Sara."How do we get in?"

"Go round the other side. You'll see a doorway."

They went round the end of a huge log between them and Katerina's voice, and found a tiny circular entrance that led — it appeared — into the very trunk of a tree. Rebecca peered in and could make out no more than Katerina's dark shape. "Your eyes'll get used to it. Come on in."

Their eyes did get used to it. They had found a crude hut built in the space between two large trunks that lay two or three yards from one another. The gap was roofed over with branches and roots. On the shingle floor were old reindeer hides — motheaten and worn, perhaps left behind as worthless. The air carried a tang of rancid smells: the hides, staleness, something indefinable but human.

A series of deep recesses had been cut into the trunk of one of the trees that were the hut's side walls. Most of these crude cupboards were empty. But in three of them stood stones large enough to be, in effect, the most solid of cupboard doors. Katerina reached up to one of the stones and pushed it. "Wedged in," she said. "How odd."

"I wonder," said Rebecca. And she pushed a hand as far as she could into a gap between stone and wood and tried to prize the stone out. Nothing moved. "I wonder." She looked around the floor and saw a short stick, some implement that the occupants had improvised out of a hardwood branch. She picked it up, tested its strength, and then pushed it a few inches into one of the stone-filled recesses. She pushed, turned, levered. The stone moved. She tried again with her fingers. Then again with the stick. Bit by bit she worked the stone loose, then managed to force it out. It fell onto the shingle below. The space behind was very deep, and dark. Rebecca peered at the blackness, then pushed the stick into the space, groping with it at the darkness. "There's something in here. Something quite big."

"Be careful," called Sara. "Please be careful."

"What do you think it is?" asked Katerina. "Let me have a go."

Rebecca poked and prodded to no avail. "I need a longer stick. No, I don't. It's coming. At least, something's coming." The end of her stick ushered a lump of something towards them. "It's cheese!"

"I can smell it!" said Katerina. "It is cheese."

Rebecca threw her stick onto the ground and reached in. "I must have broken a bit off. Yes, there's a huge cheese in here. You have a go Katerina, your arms are much longer than mine."

Katerina took Rebecca's place. She was able to catch the back of the cheese with the tips of her fingers and roll it against the side of the recess, working it towards them. "It's heavy." She panted. But now she had her hand behind the cheese. "Here, Sara, help me. Don't let it fall." Between the two of them they carried the cheese down from its hiding place and took it to the hut's entrance. Rebecca said: "Take it outside, where we can see."

They stared at what they had found: food. Blackened, not quite round, like a deformed football. Sara touched it. "It's so hard." She laid her hand on it, not so much a caress as a gesture of incredulity. "Is it smoked?" she asked, and before waiting for either of the others to answer said: "What are we going to do?"

"Do?" Said Katerina. "We'll eat it."

"But it belongs to someone. Whoever made it. Whoever hid it there." Sara looked at Rebecca, for guidance.

"We're starving to death!" Katerina shouted. "Don't you realize? We're going to die if we don't eat."

"We'll leave a note," said Rebecca. "We'll explain." She picked up a stone from the shingle at her feet and broke through the cheese's outer skin. The black peeled off. The cheese behind was very pale, almost white. Rebecca used her stone again to break off a piece the size of her fist. She divided it and gave some to Katerina and Sara. Then she broke a piece off for herself.

They ate. They ate real food — not roots, not berries, not indigestible scraps — for the first time in many, many weeks. They ate without speaking. They chewed in great concentration, searching for the nutrients in every mouthful, each of them afraid of the cramps and nausea they knew would come if they ate too much too fast. They filled their shrunken stomachs swallow by swallow, like communicants.

And they drank lake water to ease down the cheese, to help ensure that their entrails would not rebel, to soften their throats into allowing as much of the cheese as possible into their beings. They said nothing of the taste. Until all that remained of the cheese was a scatter of blackened rind.

Sara and Katerina lay against driftwood, eyes closed, and rested. Rebecca sat for a while then walked among the trees. Unseen by the others, she vomited.

Later they searched for more hidden recesses, more food. They found two cheeses and eight bundles of dried meat. The cheeses were larger than the first they had found. The meat was like withered kindling: thin slivers of leathery texture, black and frayed. It tasted of dust and smoke and, in the distance, like an essence of wild animals. "I think it's reindeer," said Rebecca.

They took all that they found and for two days ate, slept and, from time to time, splashed in the icy water. They wondered if the herders whose supplies they had raided would appear in their boats, with their herds, to collect their cheese and dry meat. Then, they imagined, they would be able to explain the theft and travel with the herders, in security. But no one came. When Sara expressed her disappointment, Rebecca said: "It's not the time of year. They'll come back over the ice, when the lake freezes, at the beginning of winter." Katerina said, "We could come then, in winter, and find them. Perhaps by then we might even be able to pay them." Rebecca said: "I doubt it."

They wrote a note. Katerina had kept a stub of pencil at the bottom of a pocket; Rebecca had a tiny notebook from which she tore a page. About to write, Rebecca hesitated: "What language, I wonder? We don't know any Eveni."

"What's Eveni?" asked Sara. "Don't they speak Russian?"

"Perhaps they don't read and write anyway," said Katerina.

"Well you can write some Polish, Sara. Maybe they'll understand that. Some one of them is sure to be able to read." Sara wrote in large, careful letters: " Drizkuję. Thank you." And under it: "My głodujemy. We are starving." They put this note in the recess where they had found the first cheese.

The next day they set off again, following the shore, making their way among the driftwood. They carried one cheese and half the meat — all that they had not eaten — in their pockets. They were stronger, but they had learnt to conserve strength: they walked slowly, avoided difficult clamberings over tree trunks in their way, and spoke very little. Perhaps they stopped less often, or stopped out of habit more than dire need. But food renewed fear: Sara had learned that the starving focus on immediate suffering, on the single problem: how to find another mouthful. No longer starving, her thoughts went forwards, beyond the immediate pain: where were they going? How could they survive? How close was danger?

But good fortune seemed to prevail. The day they finished the last crumbs of cheese and dry meat, Sara noticed, not far along the shore ahead of them, a thread of bluish smoke. They had stopped to rest, and Sara had climbed a tree stump at Rebecca's suggestion, to scout the beach ahead, to see whether they would do better to stay close to the water or look for a route at the forest edge. From her perch above the others, Sara called out: "There's someone there! A fire!"

Katerina said: "It might be soldiers. We should hide." But Rebecca, after she had joined Sara on the stump, said: "Soldiers would make a big fire. That is smoke from something small. It might be a herder family. We'll go and look." And to mollify Katerina, she added: "We'll be silent as mice."

They did not need to be silent. Two women sat by a fire, talking to each other and cooking a large pot of sweet-smelling broth. They spoke in loud voices and burst often into laughter. Sara, Katerina and Rebecca hid themselves behind a tree washed up across the beach, within easy hearing of them and from where they marvelled at the two women's plumpness and exuberance. One was much older than the other, but both were in loose, ill-fitting dresses made from fabrics of such brightness — the brightness of a world Sara had ceased to imagine. And both had scarves over their heads that would have clashed with the dresses were it not that, between them, there was too great a fury of colours for any one to be out of sorts with another. Sara gasped at the lavishness of the two strangers' clothes, and thought to herself: "They must be actresses!"

The two women spoke in Russian, which Sara could understand. She listened to the conversation that caused such hilarity. The older woman was telling of her dealings with a man. Sara heard her say: "He was so ugly, a wart, repulsive. He dared to say to me I could have the shoes. Where did he find such shoes? Satin. Hand-stitched. German, I'm sure. Such colours! How could such a wart find shoes? He must have killed for them. He must have been at the front."

"Retreating?" asked the younger woman. "Retreating you find satin shoes?"

The older woman ignored her companion's question, and went on: "I told him, they are no use to you. He said, try them on. I tried them on. A fit! Such a fit! I told him, my husband will pay for them, when he returns. He is away so often, poor lamb."

"Poor lamb," echoed the younger woman.

"Seriously, such an ugly man with such shoes on offer."

"So you offered?"

"What could I do? He wouldn't hear of money. I offered him I don't know how many rubles. You know what he did? He pulled a handful of German marks from his trousers and a handful — a real handful! — of rubles from his jacket. And then . . ." She hesitated. The other woman prompted:

"And then?"

"He stuck his tongue out!"

They both laughed. The younger one said: "And the shoes?"

"I have them at home. A perfect fit. Beautiful!"

The younger woman slapped her thighs then clutched her belly.

Rebecca and Katerina looked from the two plump strangers to Sara, wondering what was being said. Their fears were eased by Sara's smile, and they followed her when she stood up, climbed over the tree they had hidden behind, and walked out into the open.

The two women heard them, turned, stared, and jumped up with expressions of alarm. Sara saw herself for a moment as the two strangers must have seen them, and for some reason — the two women's plumpness perhaps — Rebecca's words flashed through her mind: "Thin like sticks," and without knowing that she did it, she lifted two fingers which must have seemed a placatory gesture, some form of greeting. The younger of the two women half waved in return.

Who were these two women? What were they doing on the lake shore? Did their presence there mean that Sara, Katerina and Rebecca were safe?

The two women asked: "Who are you? Where are you from? Where are your children?"

What answers did they give each other?

This much Sara learned and told Rebecca and Katerina: the older of the plump women was the wife of a brigade commander. His men had advanced to the southwest, leaving wives and families behind. Nothing had been heard from the front for two months. Before that they had lived in a small town — a garrison, a fortress — far from the war, waiting. Her husband had been at the relief of Leningrad. He had come home for a few days, then gone again. The younger of the plump women was the older one's cousin, and had stayed with her. Her family had disappeared, but she expected to find them again, in Minsk. The older had three children, the younger none. The children were in the village.

"The village!" exclaimed Rebecca. "Is there a village nearby?"

Yes, they said, there was a village, not much more than two

kilometres away from the lake. A small place. But there was food. The two women came to the lake shore to be away from the village, to bathe, to have picnics on their own.

Yes, they would look after these refugees, but it would be better if they stayed away from the village.

That was how they survived.

"And you know," said Sara, in the car. "The strangest thing of all, we did not understand the two women's concern." Sara and Rebecca and Katerina's ragged clothes and thin bodies did not merit the pity that they felt descend upon them. They looked at one another. What could it mean?

"We learned, soon enough, what it meant," said Sara. "Letters came, from the occupied zones. Jumbled letters that the two women translated to us. The Germans were retreating. Their husbands wrote of what they saw."

"You see," said Sara. "We — Katerina and Rebecca and me — we did not know that our families were dying or dead." They did not know about the ghettos, the camps. They did not know about the waystations for the death machine. They had not heard about the so-called final solution. Sara said: "We had left Europe. We had run away." They had hidden beyond its range. They had found themselves far to the east, under the Soviet cloak; protected, muffled by it, living in silence. "We just did not know!"

One day a letter came to the younger of the Russian women. She brought it to show Rebecca. She said there was good news, from the west, from the front. Her husband had met a Polish refugee who told him that the ghettos had been "liquidated." Liquidation! Turned to water, allowed to flow away, at last, into the oceans, into the past. This must mean — what else could it mean? — that the Jews had been freed, and could live again in their homes. Rebecca told Katerina and Sara.

Sara said to me: "I did not understand. I barely knew what a ghetto was — the Jewish quarter? Rebecca explained — the most simple explanations. She told me, as she might tell a child: the Germans had occupied other people's territories, and created ghettos for the Jews, even in Germany." Hesitant explanations. Rebecca knew so little, while her hopes cancelled out her fears. Prisons and misfortune, she believed, must have been destroyed.

Little as they understood, they were sure liquidation must be good, must somehow be part of the end of the war, and they celebrated. The two women brought vodka and sausages. They laughed and danced together at the lake shore. "Do you realize," said Sara, "what it was that we were celebrating?"

A few weeks after this news of the "liquidation," another letter arrived. Also from the husband at the front. A victory letter! Now he was writing from much farther west. He had heard that the Americans and the British were moving as fast towards them. The Germans defeated everywhere, in between. The war was as good as over! And now they were discovering what had been done. Comrades of his had described a camp. Russians who had been prisoners had told him about others. The Germans had slaughtered everyone, everywhere. Jews, communists, prisoners. But especially the Jews. There are none left, he said. Imagine! All gone! But for skeletons, ghostlike remains of human beings. This he described in a victory letter.

This was the end of the story Sara told me in the car, on the autobahn. I suppose I have smoothed her story here, in making a memorial. Her way of telling was slow, drifting into the minds of Rebecca and Katerina. Evoking for me, for herself, the light, the air, the moment by moment quality of those days. I did not interrupt. Until the end. I said: "What did that second letter contain?" She said, simply, that then they heard what had happened. They discovered that "liquidation" had meant something different, had been a misunderstanding. It *was* the end of the war.

Then I asked: "How did you live afterwards?" She said that the two women kept them safe. She said that Russian officials came, months later, less than a year later, when Germany surrendered. The officials asked them where they wanted to go. They could choose a place to be repatriated. What a notion! Rebecca and Katerina chose Palestine. Sara said she must go to England. She claimed her husband was there. The grammar of her claim might well have been imprecise, eliding the difference between plain conditional and future tenses. He would be there? He will be there.

"Why England?" I asked. She laughed and said: "I was weak."

I needed to stop the car. I said to Sara: "You never told me any of this before." Trucks thudded by us. I wished we were at home.

We arrived in Berlin in the early afternoon. Sara seemed excited. She gave directions, from a map we had. When we drove in England, I was the navigator. Now she called out this way, that way. Her eyes grasped at possible directions. She steered us into the centre of the west's enclave and found a hotel. We saw the great avenues, and walked by the shops — shops whose windows, to our provincial eyes, our English eyes, were a rich and elegant display. The people on the streets also: so many rich and elegant. We felt drab as well as old. Sara kept saying to me: "Look, look how they have prospered." I thought, yes, Germany.

The Lake

In the evening Sara said: "We must find the Brandenburg Gate." I thought, the great divide. She looked it up on the city map the hotel gave to visitors. It wasn't far to walk.

They were chipping at the wall, the noise of steel chisels on concrete, everywhere, like the sounds of insects. Crack, crack, crack. They had built it well. We watched them, young and old, Germans and foreigners, smashing off little pieces. I felt remote from this fervour. I thought, Sara must be tired. She tires so easily. But she wanted to walk, farther and farther, beside the wall. And all around, men and women with tables or trays or just a spread on the ground, offering bits as souvenirs. I said to Sara, "Doesn't this say it all? The cold war, being ended, its symbol is for sale." She didn't laugh. I'm not sure that she saw the point. She was more appreciative of the market economy than I could ever be.

We went back to our hotel. I was exhausted. I lay down on the bed. She sat beside me. She said she wanted to go to the countryside, to the east. I said, "Can you just drive out into the countryside?" She said, "Ask at the hotel desk."

I went downstairs to the lobby, and asked. A rather grand young woman — large and chic in a German way — said "Of course, you could drive there now. At least, no one would say anything, they hardly bother looking at your passport at the borders." Really? "Go through Checkpoint Charlie," she said. "They're taking it down next week. It'll be your last chance." She spoke such excellent English; was so full of enthusiasm. I thought, she's so different from young people I know. In Brighton hotels. I asked her where the most beautiful countryside was. "Go to the north of the city," she said. "To Rheinsberg." She said there were magnificent woods, that it was so romantic. I wondered if she saw who was asking her. "And the lake there, it is wonderful." She showed me a map, and pointed out a simple route from the city. "It is the place where many in the east have their summer houses."

I told Sara about Rheinsberg, the woods, and the lake. "Good," she said. "That's where we can go tomorrow." "We can take a picnic," I said. "No," she said. "When you go to the east, you must live off the land. We must try the local restaurants!"

That night I held her. We had not held each other, not really, for many years. Oh, we patted one another's arms. We were friends. We were always in touch. For a long time, after our marriage, Sara clung to me. I suppose I clung to her, or to her clinging. There was little enough to believe in; apart from our need for one another. But it didn't take us long, over the years, to ossify at our separate sides of the bed. Everything seemed different now. The silence, such a huge error, broken.

We went through Checkpoint Charlie. A young border guard smiled at us and waved us past semi-abandoned gates and sheds and offices, the remains of a frontier. I thought, it's not a bit like spy books. I admitted to myself that I would have felt more comfortable — with familiar excitement, more boyish shivers — if the wall had not come down. Sara was very quiet. Remote, again.

We took a huge road through and then out of the city. We turned off into the countryside. Over farmland, then among woods. I noticed the trees. Sara and I always have noticed trees together. I said: "Look at those oaks, and Scotch pines aren't they?" The trees grew high above us, on both sides of the road. And when we came to villages, many streets were leafed over. "Lime trees," I said. Sara nodded, but I thought, she isn't noticing the trees, not even the countryside. "Just imagine putting in hundreds of spindly saplings," I said. "Whoever planted them couldn't have hoped to live to see the result. It would be fifty years or more before the branches would get this size." Then I felt foolish: we had said the same thing to each other before, often before.

A cliché of being together in the countryside, shorthand for a simple sense of wonder; now, it seemed, a shorthand for having nothing new to think, for seeing nothing much. A muddle of unease caught at my throat. I looked at Sara, but could see so little, could make out nothing. I thought, I hadn't realized how I have no habit of being in touch with her. I thought, we seem to have had so little to say to one another.

The roads were empty. I drove. Sara watched, I'm not sure what. Roaming about the German countryside! I found myself wishing we were on the south downs. But Sara didn't look bored. Not far from Rheinsberg we stopped. We wanted to stretch old legs. The day was overcast. I took my umbrella.

In the village where we walked, at a small crossroads, we saw a large sign fixed to a wall. "April 1945," it was headed. "Todesmarsch." And there was a bit of a map, with Rheinsberg more or less in the middle of it.

"What's that about?" I asked.

"April 1945," said Sara.

"That I can understand."

"A death march," she translated. "It says 6,000 were murdered on this march."

I looked at the map. A route had been superimposed on the black lines marking roads. The roads we were on.

It began to rain. Rheinsberg seemed like a cul-de-sac. And there had been other signs on the roadside. "Todesmarsch"; a map showing the roads through this tree-lined countryside. I wished we were in England. We never did travel, Sara and me. I'd done my share, I used to say, in the forces. Though I didn't go overseas — we were shunted around the British Isles, a few weeks here, a few weeks there. I was in bomb damage assessment. And Sara, having survived travel, joined me. Brighton. Sussex hills. Woodlands. Though not like these German woods. I said to Sara: "Doesn't it bother you, being in Germany?" She shrugged her shoulders.

We turned round in Rheinsberg. I looked at our road map, and saw a different route back to Berlin. Through Oranienburg.

Sara grew up in Poland. On the outskirts of a small town somewhere near Lvov. Her father had been a farmer. Funny thing for a Jew to be, I once said. Not then, not there, apparently. She had three brothers. But that's about all I knew. Our family has always lived in Sussex. Farmers. I never was interested. I went in for school teaching. Maths and sciences. Though I like to think I made it imaginative: more than bomb damage assessment. We'd never told each other much about our childhoods. We always seemed to be busy.

Two teachers. Two retired teachers. And the garden. A residue for our farming backgrounds. There she was, sitting beside me in a car, driving a rainy road in Germany. Funny we had never gone to Germany before. Or Poland, even. I said to Sara: "I don't know much about you — how you lived before the war, I mean, before we married." She said something like: "Nothing of it remains." I thought: I am discovering whom I have been married to for half a century. I thought: When it comes to love, we English are nothing if not tentative. Forty-five years of discretion.

The road. The rain on the windscreen. All the woodland. I said to Sara: "What happened to Rebecca and Katerina? Did you ever hear from them?" She said: "I don't know. I didn't know where to write."

We were hungry. We came to Oranienburg. We stopped, near the station, to find a restaurant, somewhere we could "live off the land." We parked and walked. She put her arm through mine. The rain had stopped; I swung my umbrella. Rather English, I suppose. I had noticed that no one else carried one. We found a restaurant, on a corner, only a hundred yards or so from the car. A busy place, but it smelled good. We sat at a table in a corner, out of the way. Foreign places have that effect, I think: make you surreptitious. Still, I think that we felt young. A couple out on a holiday, sightseeing together, united because we shared — so wanted to share — a view of things. Seeing with similar focus. Sharing stories.

A man came and sat at our table. He had gone to the bar first. I had noticed him. His eye kept turning our way. He must have heard us speaking English. He came to our table and sat there and said, in English, "Good afternoon," and smiled. He offered us a cigarette. The room was full of smoke. Sara had already whispered to me: "They *are* backward in the east; everyone smokes." She had meant it as a joke. Then this man came and offered us a cigarette. After his "good afternoon" he spoke in German. I understood that he asked if we spoke German, and said he was sorry he did not know English. I said I did not speak German, but pointed to Sara. Then wondered: might she not want to speak German? But she had taught German. To English children, though — is that different? I needn't have worried. She seemed eager to talk.

She said to me: "He says he supposes that we are going to Sachsenhausen. Do you know what he means?" "No idea," I said. "Some kind of house?" "Saxon houses," she said. I thought, neither of us has ever been much interested by old buildings.

Sara asked the man. He answered. She was staring at him. She said, to me: "It's a concentration camp. The first they ever built. It's where the march was from." I said: "When did they build it?" She asked for me. He answered. I struggled to understand, but couldn't. At last Sara interpreted: "They built it in 1935 or '36. He can't remember which. They trained commanders there, for the other camps. They practised concentration camp techniques there. It was for Berliners. And

Russians. It sounds a bit muddled to me. But he says they took the last
prisoners out in 1945 and made them walk north. They wanted to get
them to the sea. He says they wanted to put them in ships and drown
them there. To hide the evidence." I thought, the march. The German,
realizing Sara had finished her translation, spoke again. Sara said: "He's
saying we must go and visit. He says it is most interesting. He says
there's a big museum there. To show that not everyone was bad. An
anti-fascist museum, he says." I said: "Is it open?" The man understood
my question and said in English: "Yes, yes, open. Now. Every time. You
walk." And he drew a map for us showing which way to turn. "Ten
minutes, ten minutes, you go."

We had ordered pork filets and cucumber salad. I asked Sara if she
wanted to go to this camp, to Sachsenhausen. With its museum to
show they weren't all bad. Odd place to go to discover *that*. I told Sara
I would go if she wished it. She said, "It'll be going back to the
beginning." "Then let's not go." But we went. We followed the
stranger's directions.

As we walked, Sara said: "You know, I never found out what
happened. Not really." I said: "You escaped, from it all. Thank God."
She said: "I wonder. It's strange, not knowing, in fact, what I did escape
from. I never *saw* anything like this. Hardly heard about it. No more
than you." "But I was in England," I said. "That makes all the
difference in the world." She shook her head.

I thought: when you're old, you don't press for explanations.
Nothing can be made clear. Or there isn't the time, the sense of endless
time, that explanations need, or that makes it possible to believe them.

We passed by some of the old houses of the main street at the south
end of Oranienburg, then turned into a road shaded by high trees.
Limes, I think. Then came to a crossroads and turned right, and saw

the wall. Brick. High, and topped with barbed wire. The leafy suburban streets and bright gardens to the edge of the wall. As things always were, I suppose. Sara must have been thinking the same; she suddenly said: "Anything over fifty would have been there at the time." Yes, I thought, buildings and trees and old-age pensioners.

A row of chestnuts — small ones, too young to have been there at the time — led up to the Sachsenhausen gate. At the gate a woman hired out tape recorders and information in different languages. There was one English tape left. The tape recorder had a long strap: I swung it from my shoulder and walked slowly, the tape leading me. Its text had been prepared by Russian points of view: they came as the liberators, their comrades gave dignity to the suffering here.

Sara, to one side of me, there but distant, may have been listening to the English of the tape. Somehow we both acknowledged that she had no need of it; yet her need — for information, for history — was no different, on the face of it, than mine. I thought: her inner proximity to the events this place represents means that she can look and absorb and have no need for facts — least of all those decorated by Soviet notions of history.

We walked around the courtyard, on a concrete track. This was the assembly area, the place where each day the inmates — prisoners, slave labourers — were made to stand. Once, my tape told me, for fifteen hours in winter.

We walked round the perimeter of this centre of anguish. Then the tape told me that we were walking on the various surfaces of a boot-testing track. Every day prisoners, loaded with sand to represent the conditions of war and fitted out with experimental footwear, were forced to walk round and round until they had subjected their peculiar boots to fifty kilometres. Then the same thing the next day. Walking, crawling, running, jumping up and down — on grit, concrete, cinders — putting alternatives to leather through their paces. Only the strong survived this for long. Not being made from artificial substitutes, men could not last as long as the boots.

When the tape told me this, Sara was out of hearing, a little farther around the track. I walked over to her, and told her what I had heard. No one should walk on such a path in ignorance. She listened, tears coming to her eyes, then said: "Like the shoreline. Like the lake."

From the track we were led to "Pathologie." A doctor's office, on the desk a lamp made from a skull. Beyond the office, autopsy and experiment rooms. The tape told us. Here they removed dentures and teeth. Here they assembled bits of bodies as evidence of racial types. Here they tested new "cures." Here they cut open healthy limbs to infect them with sand and dirt, to watch the progress of gangrene. Here are the tables on which bodies were laid out. Here everything is smoothed over with white porcelain tiles — better I supposed, for washing the gore. Here are instruments. Here are photographs.

The next building, farther along the surrounding wall, under the shadow of the barbed wire, is the execution room. A gallows to hang twelve at a time. More details. I switched off the tape. I said to Sara: "I don't want to see these things." I don't think she heard me. I said: "Remember that we won, in the end. Remember that it was a just war, and the evil was defeated." She looked at me but did not say anything. I thought, how ridiculous I am, with my memories of bomb damage assessment. I felt deeply self-conscious about my umbrella.

We left the shadow of the wall. We walked into the centre of the camp, the outer reaches of the assembly area. The ground was covered with grass and wild flowers. I thought: some kind of vetch, and clover. Blue and mauve.

I switched on the tape recorder. It took us to bunkhouses and then to the prison block — a camp within the camp. I'm not a man who believes in such things, but I swear the air in that compound was cold, pain ridden. The posts from which prisoners were hung upside-down, and the iron gibbets jutting from the old cell walls, and the pit into which men were thrown and left to die, could work any change on the imagination. At first I recoiled: what was it to memorialize such things? Then I remembered Sara — it was hard not to withdraw into utter solitude in such a place: one needs all one's private resources to fend off the meaning of each thing before one's eyes. I remembered Sara, and watched her moving so slowly, her body more bent than ever. She seemed withered, shrunk. I wanted to move towards her: I walked to where she was and put an arm on her shoulder, a touch, a tap. But she was absent.

We went to a bunkhouse where, in one end, an exhibit had been mounted to commemorate Jewish suffering and Jewish resistance. A small exhibit: Sachsenhausen, on the tape, pays closest attention to the suffering of communists, Russians and resistance fighters. But the images must have been enough to evoke, for Sara, the fate of her family. I thought: her people, so long forgotten, so far from her. She cried, in there, at one end of a bunkhouse in the original concentration camp. She cried with one hand to her face, the other hand on her stomach. I thought: how small she looks. I said: "I'm sorry. We shouldn't have come here." She shook her head, not much more than a side to side trembling, and closed her eyes, against all that was out there in front of her, against all that was inside. I thought: I am so horribly separate from her. But I must try to be here for her, as a partner.

We did not go to the museum of anti-fascism. We walked again through the courtyard with its boot-testing track, and out to the entry gate. I handed in the tape recorder and English-language cassette. The woman asked if everything had worked. Yes, I said, it was good. As I thanked her, I saw her glance at my umbrella: I thought, how ridiculous the English can be. And I wanted to be away, far away, from the place.

We walked back down the street with the chestnut trees, past a little orchard, and a row of pretty little gardens. Back up the Oranienburg main avenue. To our car. And back into Berlin. The next day we set off for home.

We came back together. In the boat, the cross-channel ferry, from the Hook of Holland to Harwich. We watched England approach. At first a grey haze against grey sky. Then the narrow strip of land, the flat coast. We stood side by side. Sara had her arm in mine. I did not remember the last time she had held me in this encoupling way. And she rested her weight on me. The ferry whistle blew, and a voice told drivers to go to their cars on the decks below. As the voice faded, as we were about to turn and do as told, I said to Sara: "I think it was a good thing, to go to Berlin." She nodded. I thought, yes, the wall has come down.

We drove through East Anglia, through uninvaded England. I thought, the difference between here and there is so much greater than I had supposed. Round London. South through Sussex, over the downs, back into Brighton. I thought, she is from so far away, and we know it.

We came to our house. To the garden at the back. Sara hurried out, to see. She said to me: "Look at the peonies. They've almost finished flowering. We nearly missed them." A bird was rattling from high in a copper beech in the neighbour's garden. She loved beech trees. "I can see it," she said. "A mistle thrush." And pointed.

I watched her move towards the hedge — alive enough, at the end of her life. In Brighton.

WOLF

— Nina, I'd like to tell you a story.

— What story?

— About the Ukraine. A conversation.

— A conversation?

— Between you and me.

— Is it about here? About the north?

— In a way. Somewhere in the north. Somewhere near here, perhaps.
It could be in this house. I'll make it up as I go along.

— Who's telling the story?

— I am.

— Will you put on an accent? A voice?

— I'll speak like my old cousin from Charkow. But you have a part in this too. In this story we talk to each other.

— What's my accent?

— Your voice is your voice. A nice mid-Atlantic girl.

— Go ahead then.

— I'm thinking.

— If a story has too much silence it's weird.

— OK, OK. I'll begin. I'll speak first.

— We'll call her Lobotshka.

— What does it mean?

— Loba is Russian for love. A good name for a dog.

— We could call her Lob for short.

— If you were a Russian, you'd call her Lobshka, little darling.

— Not in a new world. With English. With land.

— There's plenty in Russia. Land, I mean.

— And love?

— Not for the likes of us. We have to be here. In the Yukon. At the end of the railway.

— Ah John, my hope.

— You are the hope, Nina.

— All of us. You, me and the dog. Joshka, Ninochka, and little Lobshka.

— She's not so little. John from Russia and Nina from America. And Lob. Where's she from?

— Here, of course. She's a local. We are the newcomers. She can smell the freedom for us all.

— Do you think she'll learn a new name?

— She's only two. Young dogs can learn anything.

— She's three.

— When you come north you get younger.

— Ninochka, do you like the house?

— It's perfect.

— No, I mean the wood. The logs. We come here and live in the poorest things. There are cracks. Under the windows.

— It's perfect.

— No, no. In winter there will be cold. I remember, when I was little, my grandparents' house, it was like this, only dark, dark brown wood. Logs and cracks. I had a room in the loft. Up a ladder. And at night I would dream of tortures. Spikes piercing my skin. I would wake and it was the cold. The cold like spikes, like needles sticking into me. It will be the same here, for you.

— We're not in the Ukraine! And it already is winter. You can keep me warm. We can keep each other warm. Hold me, John.

— In my grandparents' house, it was always dark. Like this, like now. I remember the cold like needles and the dark like, like . . . wool.

— Wool isn't dark.

— My grandmother's shawls were black. She was always knitting black wool.

— And now we have yellow and blue blankets.

— Nina, can you hear anything?

— No. Not a thing. Not even the wind.

— In the coldest times you can hear the frost. We'll hear it here. Crackling. You never heard that in Boston, did you?

— We lived in an apartment. We heard the plumbing. I heard my father and mother quarrel. Cars. And fights.

— Are you afraid of the silence?

— Are you?

— At my grandparents' I could hear the fire.

— Here, the fire is in the basement. Upstairs we have silence.

— I can hear the snow falling.

— Snow is silent, silly.

— The silence is getting softer. Can't you tell? It's a silence without echoes. With snow there are no echoes.

— You can't hear anything!

— It's snowing. Tomorrow will be the first day of winter.

— Why is the first of everything always a day? If it's snowing, then this is the first night of winter.

— I can hear the silence.

— Inside your ears, you mean. The ringing. The emptiness of your own ear drums.

— No, out there.

— It's lucky we came yesterday.

— Why?

— We would have got stuck in the snow.

— So you believe me.

— I believe you. Listen. Can you hear my hand? John, don't laugh! Listen. Can you hear my hand, there, there?

— Louder than the snow.

— There.

— Much louder than the snow.

— Let me listen to your hands.

— Nina, are you alright?

— Yes.

— Did I hurt you?

— No. Why did you think you hurt me?

— I can't see you. When I can't see you I imagine you're in pain.

— Because I groan?

— Yes. And I remember how your face crumples. How you close your eyes so tight, as if something is hurting you.

— You know nothing is hurting me.

— I imagine because I remember. In the dark. It is too dark. I can't feel things. I need my eyes to feel.

— Sometimes I think men don't understand the dark. You don't have enough of it inside you.

— I am under my grandmother's wool! No wonder people don't like to smoke in the dark. No light, no taste.

— There is the glow of the cigarette.

— Is there? I would miss the smoke. Its whiteness, its lack of weight.

— Do you want to try one?

— No. I told you, it's too dark.

— I wonder how Lobotshka is. Do you think she's afraid of the dark?

— She can get out if she wants.

— Do you think she's alright in the basement?

— She has the stove. And the hatch in the door. She can feel the fire. Like a light. And hear its sounds. And outside is the snow. Snow is never dark.

— She'll be lonely. She's a town dog.

— All dogs have been in the country. It's in their blood, their bones. Up their noses! One sniff and she'll feel at home. With the stove next to her. And the stove to come back to. She'll be out there now. Exploring.

— If I know Lob, she'll be asleep.

— No. She'll be thinking: now I'm free, now I'm in a wide and wild place, now I can get away from those human beings, now I can be my own dog self. Don't you think so? Don't you think she'll be tasting the air? She's back there, now, with her ancestors. Think of it! Tomorrow she'll be out in the snow, snuffing and tumbling and coming alive.

— You're talking about yourself. You're the mongrel in the snow!

— Am I? Right now it's just dark.

— You sound a bit scared.

— We men are never scared!

— Seriously. You do. Just a bit.

— I'm frightened by its weight. I think: perhaps it will be dark for ever.

— Why don't you get up and draw a curtain? You can tell me if it's snowing.

— I'm too lazy. And you're too warm. Listen. I can't hear a thing.

— Listen to my face. Listen to the air. Listen to the shape of your fingers. Listen to all the things you can't see. Now there isn't any darkness, is there?

— I'm not sure.

— Shush. Listen.

— Nina. Nina. Are you asleep?

— What?

— Nina, wake up. Hey, wake up.

— What is it?

— I've got something to tell you.

— What?

— I love you.

— You're crazy.

— No, listen.

— I can't hear anything.

— Listen! In the basement.

— What is it?

— I think it's Lobotshka.

— What's she doing?

— She's moving about. I think I heard her whining.

— I told you she'd be lonely.

— She might want to get out.

— She can, can't she? Through the hatch in the door?

— She might not be sure.

— Do you want to go down and see?

— No.

— Then go to sleep. Anyway, all our things are down there.

— She can't unpack a box, find some biscuits.

— Idiot! She can smell us on our things. Even in the boxes. She knows she's not on her own. She's more at home than we are!

— Listen!

— Let's go to sleep. It'll be a heavy day tomorrow. Unpacking. And the snow to be free in.

— Ninchka. Are you really glad we came here?

— Yes.

— You don't think it's crazy. I mean, just coming here. We don't know the place. It seems so large. I mean, so without boundaries.

— We'll fence ourselves in. We're going to make fields. We'll cut down trees. We'll get to know it. Make it our own.

— Will we? I keep thinking, perhaps we've come too far.

— We're not in the middle of the tundra!

— Aren't we? No, I suppose not. But we are in the middle of a forest. How big is the forest?

— How big? As big as . . . as the world. Nothing between us and the Arctic Ocean. Except trees.

— Trees and tundra!

— But that's what you said you liked about the idea of coming here. Nothing but nature.

— Perhaps it's the darkness. And the silence. Nina, I can't *feel* anything. I'm, well, I'm sort of empty. Void. *I* am not here any more. I've left me behind. In the light and the noise somewhere. And now that I'm not here I'm not sure who is. I'm undefended.

— We've had a hard time. The journey. It's all new. And that *is* hard. We're strangers. But it's an adventure, remember. We couldn't have stayed on living like we did. We couldn't have survived that — all that light and noise, all that *city.* So it feels unsafe.

— It feels infinite.

— Maybe freedom is.

— And unknowable.

— What can anyone know in the silence, and in the dark?

— Hold me.

— Men! Hot for adventure until it's dark and quiet, then they fall apart.

— Don't laugh at me.

— I'm not really laughing at you. And I can feel you. I can feel you in my womb.

— Like a baby.

— In a way. And like a man.

— Nina, I've just had a thought.

— What?

— There's only one way of making love in the dark. I mean, you wouldn't want my tongue between your legs, me in your mouth, in the dark, would you? Or me on your back? You have to be face to face, feeling the other's breath. You need to be sure you're with the *person*. Otherwise you never know. That's right, isn't it?

— John. Let's go to sleep.

— What's that?

— I don't know.

— There it is again. Outside. What is it, John?

— I'm not sure.

— I'm scared.

— It's an animal. Growling.

— Do you think it's Lob?

— Doesn't sound like her.

— Listen! There's more than one. That came from the other side of the house. Do you think it's burglars?

— Shh.

— I . . .

— Shh! There. It's right in front. Right under the window. It's something fighting.

— It *is* Lobotshka! She's fighting with something.

— I'll go and look.

— Look out of the window.

— I'm trying to. It's pitch black out there.

— Is there snow?

— Yes. It's snowing now I think. I can hardly make anything out. Nina, you come and have a look.

— Where are you?

— Here.

— I wish the electricity was switched on.

— Where's the flashlight?

— In the kitchen. I put it in that cupboard by the fridge.

— Do you think you could find it? And bring it here?

— Just listen to them! It's a battle out there.

— Hurry, Nina. Bring the flashlight. We can shine it on them. Go on. Where did we put the gun? I mean, in which box? I'm going to need the gun. Whatever's out there sounds awful fierce! Have you found it?

— I've got it.

— Great. Keep the beam down. We'll take whatever it is by surprise.

— Here.

— You shine it. Straight ahead I think. I'll watch. Jesus Christ!

— John, what is it?

— It's a wolf!

— It's Lobotshka.

— A wolf's got hold of her. Christ, it's killing her!

— Lobotshka's big enough to fight, isn't she?

— I'm going to look for the gun.

— It's in the crate. Wrapped in your jeans.

— And the shells.

— I don't know.

— Give me the flashlight.

— Lobshka's lost a leg. I mean, the wolf's bitten off one of her legs.

— Stop looking.

— Oh God. John. Stop them. Please make it stop.

— Give me the flashlight.

— No! Lobshka! Lob!

— Give me the fucking flashlight! You open the window and shout or something.

— It doesn't open.

— Then go to the kitchen door and shout.

— John, Lobotshka's trying to crawl away. The wolf's got one of her other legs. It's eating her alive.

— It doesn't like the flashlight in its eyes. Maybe better than trying to find the gun. She can't survive this anyway.

— Why did she go outside? Couldn't she smell the wolf?

— Maybe she wanted to make friends or something. Hell, don't watch, Nina. Go back to bed.

— Can't we try and save her? Let's go to the door. We could shout.

— OK. OK. We can shout.

— We could throw something at them.

— Like what?

— The kettle. Oh no, oh God. Her insides. Her insides are coming out.

— It's going. It doesn't like the light. Beam it into its eyes.

— It's got her insides. It's going away with her insides.

— It must be starving.

— Maybe there's a whole pack of them.

— Shine the light around. We'd see their eyes.

— John, I think I'm going to throw up.

— Give me the light. Stop looking. She's dead anyway. She must be dead.

— She's moving.

— Don't look. It's just nerves. Spasms.

— John, she's moving. She's not dead. Can't we do anything?

— No. No we can't do anything.

— Her intestines. That's her intestines, stretched out.

— The snow's covering everything up.

— What are we going to do tomorrow?

— Tomorrow?

— We can't go out in the snow. With Lobotshka, with bits of Lobotshka lying there, covered up.

— We'll bury her, Nina. We'll dig her out and bury her.

— We won't be able to find her. The bits.

— We will.

— She'll be frozen solid. Frozen to the ground.

— She's in the snow. The snow keeps you warm.

— But John, it's freezing out there.

— Not in the snow.

— Will the wolves come back?

— I don't know. No. Why should they?

— They might try and get in the house. Try and get at our stuff.

— What stuff, Nina? Wolves don't want our stuff. They're frightened of people. They don't like people. There's nothing for us to be afraid of.

— It was so *huge*. And so thin.

— It was probably starving. A lone wolf.

— Don't make jokes.

— I'm not. A wolf on its own, kind of crazy. I've read about that.

— Then it could come back. If it's crazy.

— I'll find the gun and the shells. I can shoot it.

— Look at the snow, John. Lobshka's already buried.

— We'll find her tomorrow. Like I said, we'll dig her up and bury her.

— Is that it?

— Yes.

— That's not a story about the Ukraine. It's an animal story. Animal stories give me the creeps.

— How come?

— I care too much about them. Mention a horse or a dog and I go sloppy. And do you need to have *both* legs bitten off? And the intestines! It doesn't seem real.

— Not for a dog, perhaps.

— And you can't say "fucking" with a Charkow accent!

— Nina! Ninchka! It's a *story.* Not about dogs. About trying to get away.

— Your symbolism is haywire.

— Nina.

— Yes?

— Look out of the window.

— Is it still dark?

— It's stopped snowing. And the sky. It's getting light. Nina, let's take Lobotshka for a walk.

— I thought she'd been killed by a wolf.

— Well, perhaps you're right . . . Here there are real wolves. Timid. In the forest. Invisible.

— John.

— Yes?

— Let's have a huge vegetable garden.